I0749289

CONFESSIONS

Also by John Fraser
and published by
AESOP Modern Fiction:

Animal Tales
The Answer
Black Masks
Blue Light / Starting Over
The Case
Down from the Stars
Enterprising Women
Happy Always
Hard Places
An Illusion of Sun
The Magnificent Wurlitzer
Medusa
Military Roads
The Observatory
The Other Shore
People You Will Never Meet
The Red Bird
The Red Tank
Runners
'S'
Short Lives
Sisters
Soft Landing
The Storm
Thirty Years
Three Beauties
Tomorrow the Victory
Wayfaring

CONFESSIONS

John Fraser

AESOP Modern Fiction
Oxford

AESOP Modern Fiction
An imprint of AESOP Publications
Martin Noble Editorial / AESOP
28a Abberbury Road, Oxford OX4 4ES, UK
www.aesopbooks.com

First edition published by AESOP Publications

www.johnfraserfiction.com

A catalogue record of this book is
available from the British Library.

First edition 2019. revised 2024

ISBN: 978-1-910301-55-5

CONTENTS

1

BERNARD, CRYSTALL & VIAN

SHE'S BEEN my friend for many years, I don't get bored. She doesn't change. She's thin and warm, alcohol. We go to sleep together, she holds me tight, and some time in the night – she leaves. I look for her all day – she's like a roll of silk, a scroll – I unwind her, sometimes there's battle scenes, a warrior with another warrior's head tucked on his back, sometimes – storks, chrysanthemums, or branches of red flowers, the Judas tree perhaps. We don't have sex, but every time, she is an aftermath. I'm straight, she's she – but if I'm gay, he's a young knowing lad who grows mature so quick, until he is my *copain* by the end; what larks we've had, so lighthearted, so many pranks you skid and skip away from them, don't feel a thing, maybe some arrogant guy, he trips you, socks you in the face – no matter, you just slide away. She's my partner, with her I fear no man. I get away with saying what I think.

And I think bigger when I am with her, she's not too good for me, and that's the best thing, probably...

*

'She'll let you down,' says Vian: 'Coat your eyes with scum, and roll you for your cash.'

'Oh, friends do that,' says Crystall: 'You have to be prepared. You're alone with one – and there's a rape, a stoning, you can't prepare.... You can't worry either....'

*

'Drugs – they aren't like the drink,' says Bernard: 'The strong ones – they're like a pushy guy you meet, or else your mother.... They let you peer down inside the box – and then you're in! It isn't friends at all! The weak ones, the smokes – they slow you down, speed up the clock – who cares?'

*

Others in the group – they tell their pompous tales. They leave.

Outside, the street, it's a battle, often a surrender.

Crystall hugs Vian and Bernard.

They've stayed – 'What rubbish,' Crystall says. 'Those dreary crewmen. There they go, stumbling down the stair...'

'No,' says Vian. 'You can hide. In our little company, right here. This group – they're secret agents, international hitmen, putschistes, wizards. No one looks in a group of Sherazades and junkies. It's the safest place. Everyone confesses everything, all the time, and goes out in the street, under the cameras. Everything you've done is illegal, or on the edge, you tell it, you profess – so – no one is interested.

'In their heads – there's some idea, like when there were those communes – a guru, a spaceship come to take them, suicide, uplift, both.... People with a problem of subjectivities – too much subject, nothing to do with it, nowhere to go unless they're pulled and lifted. Something written down, or chanted. Now – it's gone collective – jihad, all exploding together, the true life lived briefly on earth – then in the basket, up goes the balloon, your kids, their kids – all the same, not time enough to grow up differentiated, but each one strong, more determined, more stubborn, more terrible, than the next.'

'Oh well,' says Crystall. 'All will change – a little while, all metamorphs. Sharing needles, sharing those AKs....'

'Those are the athletes, the warriors,' says Vian. 'The drab rest – more interesting. No one's odd now, eccentric, a bit loopy, frightening, mooncrazed. Everybody is all that, everybody has to be.'

'Warriors?' shouts Bernard – 'Nonsense. This place is flypaper. You come because it's cheap and primitive, you spend your cash, there is no work. You stay – wrong colour to be a slave – you hope the slaves rebel, they burn you in a barrel, just so's you get out. Your feet – they're trapped. Pull out – there go some legs…! You drink the nectar....'

'Flies don't drink nectar,' says Vian.

'Everybody drinks it,' Bernard says. 'Makes it – you hear the drip in every hut.'

You pay to join the group, tell your story. There's nothing else: it's expiation, absolution. A cure so's you can go on taking things without their consequences. Go back lucid in the forest. Falling down, hiding, getting caught, being robbed and being beaten, being cheated – finding, robbing, cheating, beating.

Bernard – 'I'm a saint, a thoroughfare, a dog. That's good,' he says. 'The best. You need a name. I could make discs, tell everyone.'

'We do a fine job,' says Crystall, hugging the two men. 'Having people come and tell their tales, the bad things they do to everyone. Of course, if you're off your head, you have to tell the truth – otherwise, it's fun. These guys – they heard it's hedonism, all they do in their short lives, and so, they feel they should apologise. Instead – it's fun. That's why they do it – don't apologise! When I was in Rio, every night a *forro,* close and sweaty, in and out the dance. Gossip about what you haven't got. We should do that here. Except.'

'Why?' asks Vian. 'Why should we stop?'

'Oh,' says Crystall. 'There's spies. Those plants – they don't grow, don't stand in pots, go green and brown – they're paid. In their room, they keep a uniform.'

'They won't lock us up,' says Bernard. 'What good would that do?'

'No,' says Crystall. 'They fine you, make you pay until you're sad, don't do anything again.'

Across the road, it says 'Nonstop kino'. They're playing 'The Land of the Giant Ants'.

'I've seen all they show,' says Vian. 'I know their secrets. The ants' too. We could make a movie. "Joyful Street".'

'That's been done,' says Crystall. 'Almost. Ours could be "Hangers – Life in the Closet". 'Boozing and Cruising'. We could do titles, put them on movie theatres: – nothing within! Or people walking up and down discussing which non-existing one to see. Or coming out after they haven't seen.'

'Whimsy, Crystall,' Bernard says. 'The backers sue, even so. Nothing. It's precious – but it costs you more than something.'

'Those big mouthy guys,' says Crystall. 'Alpha talk. You see them going down the mine for nuppence. All day in the dark, then up into the dark. The painters, with their little ladders – nearer my God.... Women could do all that for half the price, be idiots just like them, and swear and smoke like hussars.'

*

'I drink,' says Bernard. 'It's company. It's solitude. You, Vian?'

'Oh,' says Vian, 'I'm addicted to myself. Today the opposite, tomorrow the opposite of the opposite. How curious I am!'

'I'm dependent on you two,' says Crystall: 'I do good. Vian does bad. Bernard turns it into something interesting, he hopes.'

'Everything's too serious now,' Bernard says, 'for us to have a hand in it. Living's work, unpaid. Crystall! You have an insight – then something in your eye turns it at once into a banality, a surface....'

'Are you going, Bernard?' Crystall asks, alert and tragic. 'Out? Outside? Those aren't puttees you are fastening on?' She laughs, she cries. 'Be prudent, Bernard,' Crystall says, over and over.

'It's fashion, Crystall,' Bernard says. 'They've rediscovered spats. Spats on your legs. Leggings. Don't laugh, you idiots!' he says and laughs. 'I'm off to meet some people. I wonder who they are?'

*

'We waited up,' says Crystall. They take off Bernard's clothes – that too is what you do.

'He's lost his spats,' says Vian.

'Weren't you intrigued?' asks Bernard. 'Now, the fashion's changed.' He lies, a grub upon the floor. 'I went in, quite far,' he says. 'At midnight they bring squares of toast, with black stuff on...'

'Caviar,' says Vian.

'Oh no,' says Bernard, 'I love caviar. Then I went to this photographer's room. Silver, it was – and soot, like what was on the toast. She talked about the film, the ants. It seems there is a place that wants to wipe us out, and come and build a bigger nest, a skyscraper.... Termites thinking big.'

'Hush, Bernard,' Crystall says. She turns to Vian: 'Maybe it is time to morph our lovely Bernard. Turn him from grub to butterfly. That way he won't get eaten, and he's too pissed anyway to grasp his destiny....'

'Do as you want, Crystall,' says Vian. 'The little boys and girls – if they survive being eaten by the birds, they turn to butterflies, rise up and are eaten by the birds... Of course, they may survive as grubs, and metamorphose into birds, rise up and eat the little boys and girls....'

'So,' says Crystall, 'if you must end – and end you must – better to do it all yourself, than wait, teeter, waver, take counsel, give blood... get the sickness that you get from eating brains. You know the story – finish it! Bernard does everything – except can't take off his clothes. That's something someone always does for you. Where there is earth, you get your hole. In the country, on the steppe – your tunic is usable again. Maybe it was grandfather's? Don't bury useful stuff, and don't be squeamish – you stop needing it, and someone else is waiting. That's what they hope for – not epiphany. Your clothes.'

*

Bernard stirs: 'This is not the end, my only friends,' he chants. 'We're just at the beginning,' he says. 'From utopia to science, monkey to Hanuman. The path is rocky – better so, or it would be mud or sand.'

'That's right,' says Crystall, soothing. 'Should we put your clothes back on?'

'Far in, Bernard?' Vian asks. 'You say you went far in? There's no way in to nothing, it's all over, Bernard, and it always was. Don't be a bore.'

'Bernard doesn't look for anything,' says Crystall. 'Don't believe him. Remember Delon, the Marseille *flic*? They filled him full of wine and horse so he would be an alco, but he turned it round and shot them all. That's what Bernard wants – not the happyland – just a pal who'll drink with him, that he'll insult.'

'It's all movies,' Vian says. 'Just culture. It has no significance at all. Epiphenomenal, chitterlings, scurf, a buboe. Out it comes unforced – it takes two people, one who doesn't like to dig and hunt, prefers to doodle on the wall.'

'The kings,' says Bernard, 'were often drunk and couldn't lead the people into war. So – you must invent the state. That makes war, and lasts for ever. That's what the Kuba say – of course, it's all in the imaginary, that's why it's strong and lasts and lasts. That's what you need – an explanation for it all, for everything, how it started, how it is, how it must be.'

'It's not like that at all,' says Crystall. 'Everything you say, the two of you, the sober and the drunk – it's wrong. Those myths – they hit the bull. It's cosmology, acceptance, not a history. Everything is in the genesis. The theme – can have no variations. I listen: you both tumble down. I go along with you because I love you both....'

'Yes, Bernard,' Vian says. 'Don't be a pisshead like the rest, looking for something there is not, that you wouldn't recognise anyway. You have an inside, a dark heart, and you've pickled it.'

'Come on, Crystall,' Vian says. 'Time for bed. Your breasts – like peeled bananas.'

'Goodnight Bernard,' Crystall says.

*

'Bernie,' Vian says next day, 'these people. We hear them, their stories, try to give them different ends, more characters to speak with. The problem is – they tried to fly. Enter into myth. Some even see themselves as epic... Then down they go, drift in the street – dried leaves, bar receipts, fluff. Let's do something larger – be not so indulgent, so resigned.'

'Cash,' Bernard says. 'Between you waking them from the dream, and putting them afloat in another one – have them pay for the therapy we give.'

'Bernie,' Vian says, 'I've checked. The philosophy is good. *Es war ein Traum*. Not one, like the poet says, but a succession of them. For that, you pay – anybody would.'

'Suppose they're facho,' Bernie says. 'Those dreams. You don't want a pack of meat-cutters around.'

'If they were that way,' says Vian, 'we'd not be here, we'd be in white coats in a jail, with tasers. They're builders – some in construction, others in demolition – that's the trade: you need to know both sides.'

'It's dishonest,' Bernard says. 'The myths and epics: what we've always lived on. They're cosmology and our generic journey, challenging the dangers, making ourselves: and then – an end. Gods eternal, or a marriage and a kingdom. Happy or apocalypse, but always a fine shape. It's satisfying. It's not so. Is that really how it goes, Vian, in our lives? Who has a dream equivalent? What could we offer? Not the truth – no one would pay for that....'

'Honest?' Vian asks. 'Does that figure in the grand design? Is the universe an honest thing? We're made of stardust, Bernard – but there's no one twinkles. My plan – is make them twinkle.'

'Mutual aid. From each according to their need. We're not pros,' says Bernard. 'We share their lives, their fun, their tragedies.... Share – because they're ours, already our invention....'

'Pros get beaten by their clients. Ours – us, they – we love us, love ourselves,' says Vian. 'Otherwise – they just don't come. It's as nearly perfect as you'll see.'

'"Dream" is wrong,' says Bernard. 'Dream is inactive, muddled – physiological, involuntary. What you mean is: how you make your reality, how you live it, paint it, dance it *à pointe*. Epic realities – that's the idea. Myth – where you must climb up. Reach some top: thank God there are no gods! at the top there's only you – and up is up, wet's wet, the bushes grow with golden leaves, the birds will feed you toast with caviar....'

'Three, like us, is rather few to launch a thing – an eagle, if you don't know how, an aeroplane.... It's true, an empire starts with one....' says Vian.

'I'm lay as lay, but still,' says Bernard, 'I do the therapy. The drunks, the druggies – they are dust, not splinters of divine. And I'm the centre of our clients, their revolving worlds, the spins and slides, the trembling wills....'

'Crystall can help,' says Vian. 'She's signed on as general labour power. She goes where she is told – it's cleaning, clothes or jewels, sometimes escorts, and she does the gigs the politicos don't want to face.... Her realities are a kaleidoscope – maybe a cacoscope: instead of crumbled glass, you watch the bits of dross shift round.'

'She loves the jewels and clothes,' says Bernard. 'They suit, to deck herself when she's a minister. She reads the stuff, and frowns and squeezes hands....

'And, Vian, being in security, you know the secrets, carry arms, and know who you should shoot, who's on your side....'

'It's true,' says Vian, 'up to a point. We stand around – insurance. We don't intervene, it's just the policy says there should be guards... Of course – I know the secret state, the threats, all that, the good ideas, survival and what brings applause... It's so. I'm high up on the mast and holding on – the pirate ships, you see them far off –

and they see your own black flag, white logo and its message....'

'Crystall,' Bernard says, 'maybe she could borrow – paste jewels, even an ermine robe. Deck us out. For you, Vian, a nickelled shooter....'

'Oh no,' says Crystall in a three piece suit, flouncing up, 'Today, I'm in defence. A tall poppy's stand-in. I love the preening – it's the cleaning that defeats. I can't borrow: maybe I could beg – I'm on the flat labour rate. The agency ... it gets the rest. '

'Well!' Vian says. 'You get paid almost nothing and do all the work, you say – and every work there is. I seem to have heard it all before – maybe in a book?'

'Oh yes,' says Bernard, 'we shall stop all that. My poisonous friend, though – I'll keep her, my transparent mamba in her glass. And you, Vian, you'll go on testing all those pills and phials, see what the attraction is ... and then you know it all, the whole. All possible fictive worlds. And stop. Enough! It's just a panorama of no place, or a fever, a delirium, wet blanket or a fidget. That's what's revealed. An obsession – touching every corner of a box, or running, lifting weights. You try each trick, Vian, and good for you. Suits of armour for giant ghosts – takes muscle to wear that air. Swallow those twittering finches. The rest, the people, those who think they're sick and uncontrolled, rushing somewhere appalling, the last bad trip.... You've tried the mall, the chemicals, everything that's in the universe, refined and weighed in the balance. They come after you, they hook on. Like aphids on a rose.

'Multiple realities. That's what we can offer. And ours will be the best, the greatest choice....'

'Oh,' says Vian. 'Must we bring in choice? It rather blunts the edge.'

'Wherever there are three,' says Bernie, 'like us, well qualified, without a qualification for all the things they'll have to be, they're always being chosen, mostly they fail, they disappear. Always, though, they have a scheme. We're just the best, then, with worlds, provinces of significance, all tested out. We've been there, whatever we decide to be: telling the stories that you use when you escape, or when you want to be let in....'

'That's rambling, Bernie,' says Vian. 'Our clients don't have much choice: they can stay what they are, or be just one other thing. Burned out and lucid.'

'We three,' says Bernie, ignoring him, 'can go on a ramp. Do our big thing, live ourselves right out. But – I ask you, don't let Crystall go too far, don't sacrifice her, Vian, because you want to croak the loudest in our pond... She's gelatine – she wants to follow some parental shape ... don't make her be a victim....'

'So, she's your soft spot, Bernie! Don't cast me as the dominant,' Vian says. 'I'm not the wise guy, the most potent – I want to do good. Don't analyse me – you can't, and no one has.'

He pauses. 'I want the bad as well, of course – they go hand in my hand.'

'Right,' says Bernard. 'Multiple realities, but no greed – one at a time. Egology – self-understanding. But thereby – transcendence. Understanding's not enough –

it's the tarmac from which we fly, the canvas that awaits our touch, the keyboard....'

'It's what I have,' says Crystall, 'but with better pay. Every job is rational, it's wanting to be rational, at least. Yes, Bernard, I'll be with you. Our group – they're not searching for a cure from being what they are, but a way to explore the infinity of what they're not.... Not booze and pills that burn you out – reason, Vian, that's the aim. The project, Bernie....'

'Yes, Crystall,' Bernard says. 'But take it easy. I see you falling into contradictions, my dear heart...' He weeps, he comforts her. He comforts himself – he knows he needs it. Crystall's not convinced, when she reflects –

'I know the universe – is not built on honesty,' she says. 'Is reason what we have, so's we can know the universe – or is the reason somewhere there, in methane lakes and stfling gas – that we can find and be at one with it?'

'There, Crystall, you see,' says Bernard, sniffling. 'At once we're in confusion. Stick to reality, my dear: and make them multiple.'

Vian asks: 'Dear Crystall – when you fill in for a minister, defence or war, it's much the same – you could make war or peace? An hour's enough...'

'Oh,' she says, 'I'd not do that. I need the work.... But insults, provocation, smiles and bribes, yes, that, and transhumanism, if I understand it right... They'd vote for me, I'm sure – they like a bit of character....'

Vian turns away, he says, 'Enough! Enough to know what we might see... Of course – Bernard is pap. So are the rest – we need strong guys to take the dope, fill up with booze....'

'Oh Vian,' says Bernard, standing by. 'They do! They do! That's where you go wrong. There's the problem we must solve – how to make use of what's as venerable as shamans' drums ... renew what's always been. No one's been satisfied with one reality.... Nightflyers, virgins pure, and horses, horses everywhere.... It's one and many – how'd you tie that up with string? Reality is always in a shimmy, doubling on, and back. You must pretend there is a time and space when you aren't in the dream, a time you suffer, a time you're working for some boss....'

'It's complicated,' Crystall says. 'You'd need to know a hundred languages. I guess guys who organise the show and do philosophy – they can cut through to generalities – or else it's liquified, runs like a thousand streams and into sloughs and seas...'

They are dispirited: is it possible that something started brilliant can end so soon in rust?

'No!' shouts Vian. 'One creature – call us what you like, humans, humen – I cannot let splinter into infinities. There must be order, even if I make it by myself, and it's the order of the morgue, the torture-room, the shack, the begging-cup. The opportunities for choice may be unlimited – the kinds of choice are not. You choose among infinities of roads – then round and round you go – the globe is round, the seas are barriers, the ships follow tracks like sheep.... There's lots of destinations, and of destinies, you think – but, it's not so. Those infinities are many, so it seems, but try them out – they're finite. We're tied to legs and arms: the fins and wings, those are not ours.... Some places you would visit, others – pay to escape.'

They're half convinced. 'Bernard,' Vian asks. 'Does your hell have a name?'

'Since you ask,' Bernard says, 'it's labelled. But – you just need go up the stairs – and it's paradise again.'

'I've always wanted to go to Sorabaya,' Crystall says. 'That's romance. But – no, Vian: my hell doesn't have a name. So – I never get there, there's no one you can ask the way.'

'Exactly,' says Vian. 'Infinity it seems. A pin on an atlas, blind, but when you come to it... There's few places you want, or can. and some you must. That's philosophy.'

Is that good news? Bernard and Crystall are unsure.

'Me,' says Vian, not waiting to be asked. 'I don't believe in all that stuff. To me, the floor's all flat, so if you trip – you should get smaller shoes.'

They wait for Vian to tell them where all this is to lead. 'You dullards,' he says. 'It's not about where to go, or how you might get out. It's how you think. Then, what you see and how you stand it up and paint it, what's behind the screens and scrawls, and then who you bring on to front it all....'

'Enough!' says Bernard. 'Don't go in the deeper end. Let each our addicted friends draw on that paper what they want – paper in a roll of infinite length and varying softness, in and out of abstinence, withdrawal and all their other styles, and having statuses or not, and states and cultures, lineage and so and so ... and memories of cradles or of running, being dug in, dug out.... And then. Then, when they think they've finished, they will start again. In their brush or pencil – another face, another timpanum, another shape, a colour – as the rain sweeps up the hill....'

'It's like looking in your brain,' says Crystall. 'And seeing all the tinkling and the pearly bits laid out, that haven't yet been used.'

'Yes,' Bernard says, 'the booze and dope – they don't seem part of what we're pointing to. That's just the movie part – falling down and shooting up. How dull!'

'That is what I've said,' says Vian. 'Finally, you've understood!'

'Nothing,' Crystall sobs. 'We'll have nothing, and I'll go out to work, the same! They read a mag, these people, go to a movie – those are the realities: ephemeral, not multiple. And – they are not real, and they're not theirs, those realities. It's not enough – it's nothing, ghosts – and yet it satisfies, it's all there is. It's fraud, Vian and Bernard: illusion... What can we do? And why?'

*

'No fiddling,' says Vian. 'No implants and no scans. Do it all myself, whatever it may be, or else – there's no excitement.'

'And me?' asks Crystall. 'I'm with all of you, in intimacy, I carry you – I'm the pony on the steppe, bearing the horde. I must support you all, the panicking, the murderous, the hanged men and the suicides: Bernard, Vian – all on my back. The inflammation and the cure, I have to take the sickness on, then soothe you all, the therapy, over and over – to all of you, hitting the end wall, reeling back – and on, on again into the bricks. Or when you need to be picked up – once more into the vertical, your brains kneaded back to softness, the eyes screwed back on their stalks. Not love, Vian, it's flat rates, no contract – unenforceable in any case.... A pittance...'

*

'You wouldn't know this, Crystall,' Vian says. 'I was a revolutionary. In a party, out as heretic, in a splinter, out and in a faction, back in a party, study group, a section.... Then I realised – it was all a fantasy. When a working class is being formed – it might end doing anything. Democracy, soviets, anarchy – insurrection and armed struggle. Then, when it's settled in – maybe a union. Then – at all costs, get out, get off the bottom, out the factory....

'The myth is great – better than anything in Jung, and ethical as well. But – fantasy, Crystall. A life – mine – wasted, till I saw none of reality was unfolding as I thought... The refugees – want their kids to integrate. The blacks – want insertion. Just a few see that integration at the bottom wouldn't be so great, even if it was available. So – it's the street. Leads – to jail, of course... That's why we must find something else, another tale, another fantasy, that serves us till the end....'

'You're gross,' says Crystall, going red. 'I've never heard anything so low and crass.'

'You didn't read the books,' says Vian, ignoring her. 'The ancient ones. They didn't tell. The bureaucrats: they win, always. Orders the fanatics and the chieftains give – they lead to misery. The fanatics kill each other, and you have to parade to celebrate. Oh yes – and Bernard, our Bernie – he's finished too.'

'Liver? Kidneys?' Crystall asks, like the knowing chef.

'He's going blind,' says Vian. 'He won't see his clients, so he won't know if they're telling lies, or if his lies convince them.'

'He'll need assistance...' Crystall says.

'Not for his work,' says Vian. 'Every sense is vital. It's a solo.'

'I'd seen you as – a fanatic, Vian,' Crystall says.

'It's the wrong word – it's Ghengiz: saviour and transformer. You have to be convinced, of course, but your drive – is to save, whatever it costs,' he says. 'I'm not like that: the malleable one. I'm pliable, but I'm tempered too, I bend. 'Resist; run when they come for you. Love your friends; protect yourself.' I've many precepts.'

'There's the drought,' says Crystall. 'The cleansing. All the rest. You could commit...'

'I know,' says Vian. 'But mine's a theme – I'm not looking for disasters....'

*

'Is it good it'll happen slow?' Bernard asks. 'Being blind – means remembering, walking through your gallery – it doesn't mean not seeing....'

'Of course it does,' says Vian. 'Don't deceive yourself – you'll fall into a hole! Fast, slow – that doesn't mean a thing!'

Bernard recalls – 'The whitecoat said, "See the unicorns? Skipping in the clearing?" "Yes," I said, "Yes." "Then that's all you have left," he says. "You're finished. That's all. Nothing more."'

'Wood alcohol?' asks Crystall. 'Homemade's not always best.'

'It was bad stuff,' says Bernard. 'But in a bothy, not a wood. I think it was the tiredness. Seeing the people, trekking in the mud. And people getting sick who had no part in that, who'd never seen.'

'Too bad, Bernie,' Vian says: 'You've made it all a story, a pathetic one. I see everything quite clearly now – the things I lived through, and those that I might – give or take some years. The past – is all obscurity, of course. It's themes – those are the ideals, the only ones you'll meet in life; constructs, mental states – but solid. They stand up in your head like Maginots, Atlantic Walls. Maybe ... the stumps will always be, even though they are no use. Memory, dear Bernie: remember all your empties? – they are part of you, you'll carry them made flesh until you die. It's too bad, that now you've stopped the drinking, I have the lucidity they said you'd have, but your light's gone out! There's sure to be a lesson there – there has to be, or else ... we'd never learn a thing.'

'Well,' says Bernard, weeping as he often does, 'what have we learned? There's Crystall, working all day, unrecognised....'

'Oh no,' says Crystall, 'I'm a stand-in. I'm what people do when they are sick, or else they're doing something else... It's changed, changed completely. I'm everywhere, a substitute for something, only here today, but on the stage! I don't delve and spin!'

'It's so,' says Vian. 'We learn – the price is: growing old. Losing the will, the power to act, notching up the dead, wavering on the brink, the hole that someone's dug for us.'

'I didn't learn,' says Crystall. 'No one taught me how to be, be what I am and may not be tomorrow....'

'You're banal, you two,' says Bernard, fumbling round a table to his chair: 'Now you see – and now you don't. I made my world – it didn't link to yours, Vian. Now it's gone dark. Still mine; still being made. You can detach, and see it, quite objectified. Even – you see me. I don't see you, never, never again. I could be a beggar, blind, sitting by the dusty track – and still I cannot see you, as you see me, pass on by. Who are you, Vian? Do you leave me cash, a crust, or just ignore?'

'Oh,' says Vian, laughing, 'I think I just ignore. There are so many of you, the paths are lined – with begging cups and palms....'

‘We can’t do much for Bernard,’ Crystall says. ‘Talk to him. Give him a religion, maybe. Show him whole provinces where he could roam, without sight, a sight, a sighting. Gather groups of sightless people, have Vian explain how he himself was blind, then saw the light. And will that help him...?’

‘No, Crystall,’ says Vian. ‘It will not. But a group....! That always helps. And – to lay it out, the choice... Give lots of options....’

‘I know you try to cheer me,’ Bernard says. ‘But all these constructs – they could all be thought out by a shelf of brains, wheels in a box. Not to see – the bottles, your fellows – the stories.... What’s left in your glass. What you have to walk around ... without that – what’s the point of it? The drink? If you don’t see the scene – all is chipboard.’

‘You’ll understand,’ says Vian. ‘Taking the pills and powders – I am eagle, or I’m slug. With pills, one beast, its slither, or its glide, can’t tolerate the other. It’s delicate – there’s circles, and there’s spheres, gyres, and silvered tracks: not only movements’ rhythm, but the time it takes to pounce, to eat, have dinner, have a satisfying life.... There’s life-worlds, Bernard. Remember Crystall ... watching the clock, as though there was one time, one watcher, one effect....’

‘The clock tells what I’m paid,’ says Crystall. ‘It’s clear. When I’m a stand-in, I have the line – “War cannot be ruled out” – although I know my pulpit’s targeted.’

'You see, Bernard,' Vian says, 'it's inconclusive. Better – it's multiple. Accept your fate! Don't despair. You're still in the game, turn up your cards....'

'Exactly!' Bernard says. 'I need someone else to tell me what they are! And what's been dealt. I'll have a poker face – and there's an end to it! The others – could be gargoyles! No bets! How can I reconcile myslf...' Again, he weeps.

*

'A burrow,' says Vian: 'Not everyone who lives in one is blind – but ... it makes no difference if you are. And – to develop all the senses, when you live there, underground, you feel the shelter all around, it's not a womb, you won't be born again... What a relief! Bernard can't hunt, of course – and so he'll have his meals brought in....'

'It's genius,' says Crystall. 'I too have a thought. A shell ... not held to the ear, but lived in – a dry sea, with all its moods, without the slimy greedy shapes that live inside the wet.... Nothing to see. The burrow – you're blind, but hearing nothing. It's a grave...'

'Yes, Crystall,' Vian says. 'But a shell big enough for Bernard ... and loud...'

'Oh, they find monsters all the time,' says Crystall, still convinced. 'The giant hermit squid – he needs a shell, for sure ... to hide inside, a second home...' They laugh.

'We could build a burrow. And a shell,' says Vian.

'It seems to spoil it,' Crystall says. 'You find, you dig. Don't call a builder.'

'Everything is built,' says Vian. 'You're naturally interested in "who by?"'

'It seems easy, but it's complicated,' says Crystall. 'You send away ... somewhere. Back it comes – a shack, a semi... Then there's Bernard's blindness. All built. All structured, every tiny detail, every gap as solid as the solids it divides.'

'A text? I hoped you wouldn't start that worm,' says Vian, laughing, 'Blind and flat,' he gestures, since Crystall doesn't understand. 'They say the earth was built by worms, that everything we have, we owe to them, their crap.'

'I don't believe it,' Crystall says. 'And yet – it's soil. True. Soiled. Just a name, though.'

'Now,' Vian says, 'There's me. I can't be a soldier, though there is demand – they're still bluff and large, it's quite unnecessary – but I'm small and squeaky, weedy even. I could spy.... There's the arts – they're intermittent, but there's song and dance, and all that's in between....'

'Some people like a healthy doctor,' Crystall says. 'Others like them weak and wheezy...'

'Now Bernard's gone,' says Vian. 'We're out of cash and clients...'

'I haven't gone....' Bernard says, waving his arms, hoping to encounter some material thing, that he'll identify.

'No,' says Crystall. 'Of course – now you're always with us. Like the legions that can't see us, but we know they've been around....'

'But not to dwell on that,' Vian finishes her off.

'You could drink, Vian. Like Bernard. People will look at you – some smile, some frown. That's the two ways there are in a society,' says Crystall.

'The good thing and the bad is,' Vian says, 'no one replaces anyone. No one at all, never. I wish it was last year, when I was young, the sun put haloes on the trees, and it was the first time that I heard the birds.'

'We could make Bernard a leader,' Crystall says. 'An emperor. Not seeing gives you dignity.'

'I'm not so sure,' says Vian. 'Baldur was blind – was he divine? It was an accident. They made a fool of him. Bernard's is destiny. We can't make anything of him. He can't see what we're doing – that's a miracle all right.

'Bernard was a narcissistic hedonist, loved other people, spent his life helping them – some to find the light, others to enjoy themselves. Bernard was suicidal, with a depression so large, so well-read, well-grounded – it was enough to have it surface once or twice a year. Of course, we're all hedonistic suicides, Crystall, suicidal hedonists, condemned from our birth and the cranky people we find ourselves dependent on, to love and die, our twisty bones linked with the next old – even older – bundle on the same shelf in the ossuary.'

'Vian,' says Crystall, 'I'm the clever one. I have a wage. But what will you eat? The more you know – the less you tolerate. They'll throw you out, Vian, whoever they are. You're a mendicant. The drunks, the druggies, and the committee too – you can't curry favour with them now....'

'Then I'll curry goat,' says Vian, irritated.

'Drunks are fun,' says Bernard. 'If there isn't wisdom, often there's a joke. No one hangs around a toxic. Perhaps they should – no one asks a drunk what is his preferred drink, what gives the hardest kick. The rich and powerful, they all take different pills and powders. You should ask them which they recommend. It's dull to watch them, but, if they weren't toxic, they would not have reached the top. The drunk is modest, he won't pretend riches and power come from hours spent in the bar....'

'You're not a drunk now, Bernard,' Crystall says. 'You're not reformed. What are you, dear?'

'I might stop being blind,' says Bernard. 'You'll all wonder what comes next. I could be the hidden twin, the royal disguised as beggar... Vian's a chemist, not a proper toxic....'

'It's not chemistry,' says Vian, irritated. 'It's going to odd deserted places.'

There's nothing to say to that.

Vian has no money, and no clue. Bernard was the lighthouse.

'We'll do right by you, Bernard,' Vian says, remembering the formula from a movie, probably. 'But we have to make our track – your light, of course, illuminating, but – alas, no more. We'll make you comfortable down here....'

'Oh,' Bernard says, 'the memories! I've medals and encomia. Heroic acts and escapades – I didn't pile up memories to have them dissipate, leaves blown to all corners. I'll be back! In fig! I'll turn all that I hear you do, back into pictures on the scroll....'

'We'll leave food for you, Bernard,' Crystall says. 'Milk, eggs and olives. Shapes and textures you can recognise. Alas, the fun you had....what use was it, what profit? Where is it now?'

*

If you've heard about it, it's easy to request the operation. Along with your sight, you get a chip that lets you, when you've nothing more in mind, see shots of Bilbao, Harbin, Kiel – all the romantic places you'd not been bothered to frequent when you were sighted.... Direct to your brain. 'Now,' says Vian, 'That's multiple realities. It's been done...'

Bernard objects: from eye to brain, it's a particular route, quite personal. You see only what passes into your head, and then it's 'you'. 'Everything I see,' he says, 'Like everything I remember, is mine alone, shot from my angle, with my will, my purpose.'

'What's a movie, Bernard, then?' Crystall asks.

'You haven't understood,' he says.

Like the Bantu drunken king, the blind god whose name he can't recall, not one of the hundred of the names, or more – Bernard's locked in himself, deluded that between the object seen and seeing eye – there's a link that maybe creates, demolishes, gives life and death.... Maybe there exists a continuity – that Paul Cohen said could not be demonstrated...in mathematics? Perhaps in learning?

In everything? No – maybe not....

*

'Bernard's gone,' says Crystall. 'Now he's clean and resurrected, he's tutor to a prinitive band. Indians! – I know! A mistake in history – geography.... People deep among the trees. It is his new, eternal life. No one knows where, or when what happens, happens to him.'

'Of course,' says Vian. 'So many things that fall on you. But, Crystall, I've a thought. I'm not lovable. Broadly, wouldn't you say that's true?'

'Oh yes,' she says. 'But even people who are lovable – it's a tremendous strain. Then they hit adolescence, and the game is done.'

'It's right that Bernard, now he sees, should start at the beginning. Or – perhaps it is the end. In any case, for sure it's right,' says Vian: 'It's helping people – you can't go wrong. You know, I've tried lots of drugs, but they never hooked on me.... they were all miniatures of me, but as the original full-size, I could do better by myself. It wasn't for pleasure, or escape – just to see if any added on to what I am. None did. Of course, I tried them out – update the group ... but those guys took it differently. For them, addiction was the paradise you need be dead to enter in, and so – be very very careful.... Often, though, they weren't – not dead, not quite. I wasn't like that, not at all: I didn't do anything for real.'

'That's rather terrible, Vian,' says Crystall, though it can't be a surprise to her. Besides – she's never liked good times, the strange stuff going into her.

She'd never really say her country was at war, though people would believe her, rush to stock up, tape the windows....

*

In the jungle, Bernard's coughing keeps them all awake at night – all villages are similar, and the cough, maybe an overture to death, is a small inconvenience for when you help – although he can't restore the hunting and the animals that there were.... He'd protect the creatures too, if they had been around. His message was 'shoot first', as if anybody ever did otherwise, if they only had the means. The language – it defeats him. He used to be quite fearless, now he's scared, all the time. He passes it to everyone, the fear, or maybe it's a circle they are in and that's where he belongs, and the fear is fresh bacteria he's brought in.

You have to sort things out. The world that comes to what, in mathematics, is a premature conclusion. The robots, getting ready to do Crystall's jobs. Bernard in the clearing with people in a listless dance around. They shamble, though they've not yet discovered fermentation. Getting pissed, for them – it happens quite by chance, a fruit ... the good and evil, making sauce together.

Sorting it out, thinks Vian: that's the first lesson, getting straight. Being useful, in a way it means you're helping, whether you're a spy, or into martyrdom like Bernard.

Bernard's the only one among them who can see beyond the trees. The Indians – their eyes are bricked up, Bernard was given two tin eyes, they locked his arms, so he can go out in the sun, aim with his gun, sharpshoot without a quaver – and be a target too.

That generation, which holds those three – it's almost done. No more children to be had – be content with what you have, and if you've nothing, be content with that as well.

Bernard – who knows? He's not there now, that's all that anybody knows.

Vian – there's a limit to how bad one person is. Leave out the massacres: Vian's a good bad person, all in all. He does bad, very bad, to some, and quite good to those who pay him never quite enough...

2

SABINE, SYLVAIN & CORINNE

'IF WE FANCIED each other, it would be incest. I don't much like you. That means it would be no fun.' Sabine goes, 'Shoo! Shoo, cat. You're not mine. I'm leaving. Try somewhere else.'

Leaving – stick to that explanation – it's the best. If you can....

She packs some more, false things, in case some wear out, travelling around.

'If I wrote music, it could be uplifting – or memorable, a memory,' Sylvain says. 'People remember the tune from when something important was going on. Then they forget the important thing. Any kind of book, though – no uplift, and no sound. It's odd. People don't have ceremonies with a sing-song now – unless you go to church, and then it's strumming, or an organ in spate, a salmon ladder.... But music lingers in most heads.'

'That's all wrong,' Sabine says, abstracted. 'It's true most books are like a dolls' house – tiny worlds you can peer into, and feel huge. But people often gather to hear music, or shuffle to it. You never do that if you read a book, that's true.'

*

'Oh, I'm sure I'm Vian's,' says Sabine. 'He was addicted, hooked to everything he did or thought. It couldn't be knocked out of him. Great ambitions, great frustrations, grand malice. You must be Bernie's, Crystall's revenge against Vian. Bernard's was the weakness of sharing, adding suffering to his weakness. Empathy till – *j'est l'autre*. The man becoming his lover one day a week, then every day... His great passion – pushing broken people to be his friend and seek his protection. Not really friends, not really broken – just pliable, bending before their will to surrender. Then to his.'

'What's weakness?' Sylvain asks. 'Searching for the nothing which is your centre, your origin: the instant before you find it, there's the something you've made, you are. From nothing, the universe of you. Next to nothing is the atom, the whole chain – the something. That was Bernard ... sacrifice, protection. The tiny straw, twirling in the vortex. Vian – was full, full of everything he could swallow and inject – all to show he could take it all, it made no difference, he could resist, good, bad – it was all the same.'

'The three rooms they left,' says Sylvain. 'They make a house. Look – there's big trees outside: – wherever we travel, the best you get is little trees in snow.'

*

'There's no airport here,' says Sylvain, as they land. 'It's too near a frontier. Two frontiers.'

The cops stare at Sabine. 'She's the image,' Sabine hears one say.

'I'm not related to her or anyone,' Sylvain says.

They're taking Sabine somewhere no one wants to go.

'You bastard,' Sabine shouts: it makes no difference if he is. There's no comrades now, no sacrifice, no greater cause – best skitter out those doors before.... You're out! Bielorus? Ukraine? Russia? Another? Ossetia? You'll find out!

*

'Avoid fine phrases,' says the guy. 'Anything you read, see on TV – you may emote, but it's just lines, black or in colour. Keep it simple, flat. Don't pretend you have real feelings for the images... That, friend, is idolatry....'

'The image was of a resemblance,' Sylvain says. 'Probably the cops remembered – someone they were told not to forget. The father escaped them – so they caught his genes: Sabine. The sinful fathers die, go to hell, then comes the next generation, off it starts, the new's the old. Only a half mistake.'

'Your problem,' says the guy, 'it's the world's gripe. Don't bother me, though – this kiosk sells ciggies, nothing more.'

'Oh,' Sylvain says, 'it's a relief – just talking about it, a disappearance....'

'If a thing's gone,' the guy says, pushing Sylvain away, buttoning up the stall, 'It will not return or – maybe it will. That's all that can be said.'

Got a story? Best, if you want a sympathetic hearing, avoid the uniforms: a guy with a stall, usually they listen.

*

'The document you want,' says Sabine. 'I don't have it. It does not, cannot, exist. If it lets me off, or condemns – I can't produce it. Is it so important to you, or....?'

'It's vital,' says the man in jeans. 'But not important – how could it be, if it can't exist?'

'I didn't want to be here,' says Sabine. 'I'm going west, where there are birchtrees....'

'Everybody looks for trees,' says the man. 'No one wants to be here, not me, for sure....'

*

'They're so beautiful here,' thinks Sylvain. 'More beautiful even than in Budapest – they don't let anyone leave, so the women stay, don't marry rich old men or poor young ones. And the men – I guess they're beautiful too. Bernie the beautiful, left me that sliver of being gay, an operatic cadence, no more: enough to like a picture, vermilion, a frock – enough to raise a hope, but nothing more. Best to leave Sabine where she is – "We didn't mean to come here – though," she'd say. "We have no destination..." or rather, we all have one, but it is hidden, like the imam, the secret, the key to the kingdom, and for most, as we slither down the ashy slope, we'll never clutch that golden key, nor will cops for sure, nor me.'

'No, best that Sabine wears them down – it's all bad turns inerited from Vian: if you don't believe in sin, original or just derivative – who cares what her father did…? Except, of course, here, they believe in sin, original and re-invented. Believe in it lots, and every hour, and every one. And – suppose I am Vian's son? That would be the highest card Sabine could play.... Trade me for her.'

'Hey, my friend,' says the tobacconist, catching up – his is a dangerous life, his trade more lethal than jihad or walking on the clouds... or selling Ducatis.... 'How do you live, travelling around...'

'Oh,' says Sylvain: 'I and my sister – we fix things.'

'What things?'

'Anything that we can fix,' says Sylvain – the path's familiar – 'that can be fixed. By us. Don't ask to fix your country, if you mean – make it a good place. We fix, but we don't polish, we don't paint.'

'That's radical,' says the guy. 'To fix what's wrong, you have to start at the beginning, at the root. Maybe you don't make it perfect, but ... all the same, you put it right. Creation – or destruction. Vision or mist. The flame – the snuffer. The coil, the strike; the lurk, stalk, tension – then the spring, the throne that rises, or the palace flattened, and dishonoured...'

'Machines and systems – those are easy,' Sylvain says. 'Timepieces are fiddly, necklaces – leave them run about the floor,' and he laughs.

'I've old broken stuff...' the guy begins... 'Then throw it out!' Sylvain shouts, laughing louder. 'If you've no cash and can't replace – throw out all you can, live lean, enjoy the space. We're like the teams who went around sharpening knives, patching umbrellas – the vengeance and the refuge....' and he laughs more, pulling the poor guy, this tobacco-executioner, pulling by his scarlet nose, so many pink vestas struck thereon – sets out the spiel, all Europe fixed, Poland – a snip – and on and on, fixing the Donbass, fixing the peoples of the steppe, the tundra – then, you start again, fixing the Navajo, the Sioux, whatever you can find, Ojibwe, fixing the dolphins, round and round – a modest fee, rooms with a basin, cold water, a dried brown fish slipped in the backpack, on and on, until ... it all comes round again..

'Your partner,' says the guy, 'she didn't make it through the customs....'

'No,' says Sylvain. 'Customs is what we cannot fix.'

'You see,' says the guy, 'with my trade – I'm a *passeur*. People here – they can't leave. They can leave – but then they disappear. They're nothing, once outside – they're easties. They clean but they are dirty, they dirty, but their spirit's clean, burnt in the fire... They can't leave, so I pass them to the other side, the other shore. It's their spirit, their breath, the *pneuma*. It sounds like wheezing, stifling – it's not. It's the sound the steppe makes, the wind, the stiff mist – you hear the pony with its laboured breath, the vast horde of ponies, hidden in the white. I help the people – here, not here, with the *papirosi*, the *toscani*, the cheroots – easing their spirits, out and beyond, up and still rising. You and I, Sylvain,' he says, almost weeping with insight – 'We could be a team....'

Sylvain recoils: 'No, no – no, absolutely not. I help things continue – yours is what I hate: addiction. The love of death, acceptance of the greater force – surrender. My father....'

'You must be radical, Sylvain: remember, 'You are so beautiful'....? Isn't that Faust? The root of man is ... woman. The root of woman – is man. All the same, it doesn't sound quite right. "The root of man is man,"' says the tobacconist. 'There! That explains it all – the conquest, the murders. The important thing, in my work, Sylvain, is when they're gone – they don't come back, ever.'

'I quite see that,' says Sylvain. 'But that's not the work we do.'

'You said it, Sylvain: "creation – destruction". It ends in smoke. What's fixed, it's what's lit,' says the guy.

'Ah yes,' says Sylvain, 'But you're a metaphor. I've met your sort! You suck me in, Mephisto, I'd be your baby, drinking your brown milk from your dark insides. Sabine and I – we're bound for the white, the green, the herds, the hordes – the new cities standing in the permafrost – a new “forever”. New people, like we were promised – those new men, new Soviet men and women ... now, it’s the real New, whoever they may be. Then – there’s Sabine, sequestered.... I don’t believe in souls, but get her out, I’ll pay with mine....’

‘No one believes in souls,’ the tobacconist says. ‘So, they come cheap. She’s sold hers, and mortgaged yours. A soul – no longer tilts the scale. But – the gesture counts, I guess. You’ve nothing more that has a price here, or, as they say, a value.’

‘Leave it,’ says Sylvain. ‘It’s not the case. Forget all that.’

‘If you’re artists,’ says the guy, ‘there’s something there that will not die. They say.’

‘I don’t think that’s what we are,’ Sylvain says. ‘When you travel round, you pick up bits of disconnected stuff that people rather wouldn’t hear.’

‘Ah,’ says the guy, ‘you’re not artists, then. People listen to them, if they’re alive or mostly dead. Just having an awkward attitude, a look that’s insolent, or knowing – you’re identified. You can’t do proper work. You’re not artists, but pains in the arse you are!’

‘That’s what I’ve been saying,’ Sylvain says. ‘That’s why we want out of this place – it seemed quite orderly, not especially a trap....’

‘It’s very orderly,’ says the guy. ‘But order’s not the reason for the order, if you see....’

‘I think we’re nothing special,’ says Sylvain. ‘Just *intelligenty,* like everybody, almost.’

'You try hard,' says the guy. 'But that's not the language here, you know.'

'Knowing the details, even the landscape, doesn't always help,' says Sylvain.

'Work and politics,' says the overpowering, rather sinister, guy. 'They've gone: no longer in your head? Now, it's just anxiety for Sabine. You do feel, feel anxiety? Until you've no room for more?'

'Feeling's part of what we do,' says Sylvain. 'Sure.'

*

'They let you out, or else they don't,' says Sabine. 'It's like hospital. Except they all have big moustaches – if you wait long enough, one without comes and lets you go.... You've been at the brandy, Sylvain....'

'There's a bottle on every table,' Sylvain says. 'Now we can move on. And we may be in luck – the guy with the ciggies sells lottery tickets ... see....'

He has a roll of them.

'Don't hope,' says Sabine. 'We can't fix anything here, we shan't be paid off with tickets either. I only fixed my exit, nothing more – I made promises, of course. All faults from the past ... they think I have a panoramic vision ... a memory, some guilt. I just had a relative, perhaps....'

'Fixing is tough. The tobacconist didn't think I was an intellectual. He's right – intellectuals who went high up and flew – all bourgeois,' Sylvain says. 'Maybe they fixed – I doubt it. Only in history was there a progressive bourgeoisie which sometimes wanted deals with guys who worked for them. Treachery, perhaps: – in any case, the revolutionaries – all bourgeois in their thoughts, most in their origins – died out. A unique social phenomenon, all gone, Sabine. Now – no intellectuals – all is an intelligentsia. Bright frustrated guys who go to school, then do their job and afterwards – some weep. It doesn't matter what their fathers did, Sabine. Fuck their fathers! Intellectuals? – remember Sorokin – his father painted icons....'

'It *does* matter, Sylvain,' Sabine says. 'Think of Vian – a meddler, and a spy. A father, probably. I suffer, that's his legacy – and here, or anywhere, we can't fix anything that's big and lasts. We leave a sketch of how it ought to look – it's fixed, but only till it breaks again...'

'Oh Sabine,' Sylvain says, 'everything goes on till it's forgot, and then it comes again. Nature, not nurture, rules that roost.'

'Multiple realities,' says Sabine. 'They are available. It's the one big one, though, that matters above everything: – you touch it, it can fall on you, it's there, and needs no explanation.'

'Tickets, Sabine,' Sylvain says. 'Where do we go? Wait for the draw? Or fly somewhere, somewhere, things we can fix...?'

*

'These drumming schools,' says Sabine. 'I never saw so many....'

'A woman, running from the Yakuza – she took me in, fed me,' says Sylvain. 'Those Japanese drums, make your soul shudder. A depth, a deep. People want satisfaction, she said. She knew I didn't: gave it up. She was beautiful, of course, or she'd not be on the run....'

'You should have stayed,' says Sabine, laughing a little.

'Oh no! The noise, my dear!' says Sylvain laughing heartily. 'You can seek satisfaction outside. Most people think it's inside, inside themselves. Outside is best, more likely, but only the stupid ones look there. I don't need look, Sabine.

'Best be a joke like you. Entrap some guy – then you're in your trap as well, you have to dump him, you leave everything behind... Who's won? It makes you strong, untrustworthy. You should learn – work for both sides, the in, the out, the cruel, the soft: the complacent and the insecure... Then – make up one's mind, but don't let on! That's how it's done. You can do it – you've still got the tale, the plot, a breath of it at least: sex! Your string of cash. Me – I have to be a hermit, an ascetic. All I can have – is mystery! Who's buying that?'

And they both laugh.

*

It rains and rains.

'Maybe the dam will break,' says Sylvain. 'That will give you something to do.'

'It's too symmetrical,' says Sabine. 'Faust didn't build – he made the measurements: the lie of the land. Nothing about the sky breaking its promise.'

'It's the slides,' says Sylvain. 'The funicular's come loose. I'm not climbing up and down. When you're young, it's the people that's dangerous. When you've grown, it's the mud, the fear of ending under it.'

It rains and rains, and when it stops, they buy the tickets for the train. They didn't win the lottery.

'Mud on the tracks,' the sign says.... 'Months to wait...' says the guy. The stanchions of the funicular stand askew.

They camp out in the train.

Sabine hugs Sylvain: she says, 'I'm sure you realise – they took me off the list. They put you on. That's what I said – they didn't need believe but then – I'm quite convincing....'

'It makes no difference,' Sylvain says. 'If we journey on together.'

Of course, it does.

*

A guy, not the tobacconist, though he looks like him, brings tea – a nickel hump upon his back, a beak – pours tea, and, sometimes brandy. Sylvain tells Sabine – 'Beneath the brandy taste, there's something more – it must be meths, or something that flows on....'

'Spying, helping – it's all much the same,' she says. 'Knowing things, seeing intentions cause a plan to grow out wrong ... and in the end, like at the start, it turns out much the same. Bernie and Vian – the humanist, his gun: the opportunist, choosing a side he's loyal to – some of the time. The only thing that makes us differ, Sylvain, is the addiction. Otherwise, our patrimony makes us one. The tricks are slightly different, outcomes – largely chance, intentions ... acorns to the pigs, I fear.'

'Of course we're one,' says Sylvain. 'Everybody is. Maybe every thing. Just don't say so, Sabine – it's a thing you can't believe, you musn't say. Besides – it isn't true. The eagle eats the albatross, Loïc shoots the eagle, lots and lots of them, and then he eats the sheep he's saved.... If we were not the same, Sabine, we'd be immortal. The chain of being holds the bucket in the well – it's hierarchy in place, it works so you don't die of thirst, but all the rest....'

'I didn't mean all that,' says Sabine, hugging him. 'Why not go up and help them test the cage of the funicular ... it's finding out, and helping, and it's suicide....'

So Sylvain does. Top city's joined to bottom city by a cord – they're twins, inseparables, master and slave, the soul and patron body.... He steps into the cabin, and the top guys let him down...

You don't want to go in the box, you don't trust them. They josh you, you can't resist – you can resist, but in the end you go, it's a male thing, a female dare, and there are poles rigged up like jury legs instead of pylons, you pass the first, and then it falls, you, the box, the cage – end over end, like an old long-case clock with weights on chains, a brass roundel, weight soldered to the pendulum rod, and all three leaded scourges winding round your head – the box is clock and you are clock as well – a single strike and shouting from above ... you should accelerate, but each time you hit you partly lodge so the time it takes to fall is measured out, and then the motion changes, now you accelerate, the box rolls faster and faster like a seven-sided gadget that generates randomly the numbers you can stick to anything – and there is green and blue and rusty clay, and that's inside the box, and outside it is much the same, until it comes to rest in bottom town where all is quiet and you are numb, your inside and your outer shell are tumbled into one, and that's true too for the in and out of what the cabin was, the cage, the box ... all split and opened out.

*

'We're both lucky to be alive,' Sabine says.

'Don't give me the crap about being one,' says Sylvain, irritated. 'You stood and watched. You weren't threatened, you weren't in the box, the fall. You didn't think to help the guys, the engineers who's stuck the box, the cord together, called for a volunteer ... that was me, only me, not you at all.'

'Of course,' says Sabine. 'That was just you. But I was in the customs. There's no procedure to get out, you can't fall and hope that you'll survive. You must have seen the cage would fall....'

'Maybe I did,' Sylvain says. 'It moved things on – the train....'

'Is where it was,' Sabine says. 'Yours was a selfless act that hurt and profited no one but yourself. They could have done an empty run....'

'Oh, there must be someone there inside the car, to give emotion and intent,' says Sylvain.

'Well,' says Sabine, 'I have a wider, deeper thought. Monkeys are on the left, it's clear. They cherish those in need, and chase out the disreputable. But – they are patriarchal, all of them. They have a chief. Maybe they've transmitted that to all of us.... Now, though – I've found a band of them – rotating leadership, elections, all of that. I'd study them, isolated though they are....'

'It's suicide, dear Sabine,' Sylvain says: 'There's always other monkeys round, men, rhinos – all the shoot. There's no way out for us, Sabine. No primal scene, no untamed garden, fruitless, no serpents lurking there, smug with their ethical intelligence... Bernie and Vian – those were our extremes, the benefactor and the spy: bad ends both made; one put down by his fellow men, the other by a nature bold, untouchable – his organs turning on themselves – autophagy, it's called... Eaten up, alone, all by himself.' He wrings his hands.

The train is motionless.

'Leave them be,' says Sylvain. 'Monkeys. They don't mind if they're extinct. Besides, our hunting fathers – they protect. Protect and eat – that's the motto of the primitives.'

'You disgust me, Sylvain,' Sabine says. 'It's the new hunters now. Anyway – who knows when the train moves...'

'People all take the buses,' Sylvain says. 'They go up the line. We're stuck, Sabine, although we won the lottery. They don't pay out to strangers – *étranges étrangers* they call us.'

'There!' says Sabine. 'We're free. No movement here – so, we must move on by ourselves.You took your tumble: now, my monkeys – they await. We must go into modernity, Sylvain, although we know that in the end we're obsolete, our skins dry out like we are hung up on a door, we pee as if we've dined on apricots, our gums fall back like guardsmen fainting on parade, the nose juts out, a quill; the cheeks, a map of – terminus, the grimy lines all end up in their designated space ... the *capolinea*, the depot ... once we had a hole all to ourselves, now it's a bottle you refill with dust you name after who's made you pay the ritual ... free thinkers all, with no conclusion, brain anarchy, that's all, Sylvain – no peg, no spout, no beak to hang our baggy selves upon – just sprawled, then straightened, then the flame, and then forget, forget – ah Sylvain! the delight of emptiness, of nothing on the slate....'

'You'd have monkeys, Sabine,' Sylvain says, turning away from Sabine's tears.

'Surely we can ask someone, Sylvain!' she pleads.

'Who?' asks Sylvain, turning to tears himself. 'Who? Explain, advise? Means and ends? How to discriminate? How to get somewhere? Are we the right person anyway? It's a joke, Sabine... Ask Bernie or Vian. Ask Crystall, "Have children out of spite – maybe they'll find an answer..." The God here says, "How should I know? Use your brains," the other God says. "It's in the book – but the book's not about you or anyone, or anywhere, it's about everyone, irrespective...." It's like a tale written by a stranger, about no place, no time, with names you recognise but when you go there – they don't look the same... Like postcards – Berlin in 1920, Moscow in 1930 – someone's changed the production, the scenes, the actors....

'Maybe my fall's jolted me up, Sabine. I wanted space, grass – riding all day to reach another flat place that looked exactly like the one I'd left ... freeing my mind – but now I want cuirassiers, chancelleries: the electric abacus. Faust's engineers, Sabine, I need to see them drain the swamps – doing the job better this time so it works and doesn't flood or parch... Then, of course, there is the devil. He has an answer, tells you what to do. He has the history book. But – it's all about His plans. He doesn't love you, Sabine – He's your lawyer and your cop. You are His case. Will you do all He'll accuse you of? His contract comes to you in the mail, He says ... who's ever seen it? You trust Him, naturally – but it isn't up to Him, it's up to you.... Vian saw that – best take the cash, the sovereign is round, it rolls away, another head is struck up after every sliced-off head. Spend, Sabine! That's the only thing we know that works....'

*

'Hey!' says the guy, maybe he's a railwayman, the good heart of the working class, his timepiece lets you keep your job, go back to your bed, and off to work again! and on and on.... 'Hey!' he says again. 'You two, probably you're twins, a-snivelling here – and yet one's bold and foolhardy, Sylvain: the other, kind, adventurous – dear Sabine, my beautiful, my love....'

He holds her tightly: she's uncertain. Maybe he's ignorant regarding courtship, or too knowing when it comes to sex.... He has a number on his badge: 'That number, friend,' she says, 'is what I'll play in every game – it may mean luck for both of us. Our saviour....'

It's all much more than he expects – or that he needs....

*

'The brain,' says Sabine. 'It seems to override the rest, the history, the landscape – an instant biology seems to be everything, an electronic gadget, that explains the actions, the intent – but what is in our brains? Have we searched, gone far and deep enough? There was a beginning – trees, asphalt lakes, black skies. Those stayed within, in everybody's head: sometimes out it comes in poetry. But – birth, Sylvain, is not the start. It is a spasm, then in a short while, from larva to tattered moth – we die. All that we are and know – it started long ago and sedimented, so our conscious life is just an envoi, a farewell – "hear out my tale/ then leave and have your fill of ale" – a twilight couplet.... Monkeys in business, Sylvain – us: the trees are in our heads – they make no difference, we shan't climb them now, not ever more....'

'Yes, yes,' says Sylvain. 'It is familiar. The clever guys – have overweighted biology and chemistry. Instead, your brain's an epic, you must go deep, and meet with guys and read the parchments and the birchbark, listen to the sagas in the caravanserai –' he waves his hands – the story is too big and too banal to say it all – 'but, Sabine, why have you returned so soon? The monkeys? All the fuss we had of leaving, getting off the train, escaping the railwayman who fancied you...?'

'The monkeys?' Sabine asks, 'Oh, for sure they're hanging on. My first day there, the primal jungle, there's a big stream, a river in a hundred parts – a thin boat, outboard, going very fast, and four grey pigs, stood in file. Nothing good would happen to them – they all stared straight ahead. It was so sad.... What could I do, dear Sylvain? What was my role there?.... In the end – it's cash. It costs to save a species, build hotels and hostels, sell some trees to save a bush, a flower, and make a plan that fruits. It's banking and finance, Sylvain – those monkeys have a price, you can invest in them and all the province round, and in the end they die, they are extinct. Maybe they die, they're not extinct – the value ... seems indifferent to how they end and what the ticket costs to watch them squabbling and hunting fleas.... And when they're gone – the land is yours, the gold, the alum and the chrome...!'

'I know,' says Sylvain. 'I'd heard all that – what can I say?'

*

'I'm an advisor,' Sylvain says. 'The powerful guys – they're tight with cash, although it's mostly not their own. What stimulates – is fear, fear for their lives and their tranquillity, so they want soldiers, but – the soldiers cost, they're not trustworthy, so it's best to have a band of cops instead, and missiles you can fire from home. You're right, Sabine – it's all finance, putting a price on everything and hoping it will turn out right or that you'll die before the end. Spying, contraband: a bank? It's all the same. Follow the mathematics and wear a tie. The Jacobins have gone – now, there's the Directoire, tomorrow comes Empire. All that's wanted is good information, that you sell. The better stuff you keep yourself and bet or salt away as best you can. It's all respectable – once, spies ran a risk, now you gather information as a prof: soldiers and guns, and stores of monkeys too ... you do the sums...'

'It all sounds nothing,' Sabine says. 'And the people you must meet! Your dream – the steppe – it's gone, of course, but what's now? Power? Not yours. Rich and anxious – that's how you will die...'

'But, Sabine,' Sylvain says. 'You've nothing. We agreed – everything's encysted in our head, before our birth. Vian and Bernie – they don't enter in. They're links in the chain, there's no weak spot, it's not a funicular from up to down and vice versa – these chains don't break – they finish, that is all....'

'Oh,' Sabine says. 'I'm not an idiot. I did bring something back,' and there's a coach, comes to the front of Sylvain's building, where he spends some time. There's frightened faces looking out. More refugees.

'Worth millions,' Sabine says. 'You don't need a zoo, and as each one dies, the rest are worth much more. Much much....' she says dreamily. 'I brought a troop with me – look! the driver. Just for show, of course – he has a stick, can't reach the pedals with his feet, though for him, the tool-craft is a strain.... They don't let the females drive – perhaps they should....'

The troop – it clambers down, runs up the trees. 'There!' Sabine says. 'They'll get accustomed to the pomegranates here. Each specimen is tagged, of course, I hold the code....'

'That's logical...' Sylvain begins.

'Your trouble, Sylvain,' Sabine says, 'is you're soft, You make soft compromises. "People," you think. "Maybe this one, maybe that one" – forget it! People take what they want and can. The rest is stuck in the funicular car, or on the train. It's timid of you: – trying for a deal, not blasting off, not asserting to make your point. You're afraid to win, afraid to lose.

'Live in one room, Sylvain – why have two? Throw out the books you've read, and those you won't. The house back there? Give it to jihadis – see what they're worth – can they defend it, keep it clean, be neighbourly, have pets, patch up the stucco – if they can't, then dynamite it! If they can – shop them, let them face a siege.... Are they worth something? Can they make us all suffer, putting back what we have shaken off – a trauma, that: off with the old rules, let's find some more ... no! Nothing must be exclusive, there is no shame, no discrimination over anything at all. Chivvy it along, Sylvain, nothing lasts for centuries – things that don't work go on the tip. Like us: but in our time.... To everything, Sylvain, there is a reasonable response, a moderate reaction. So what? Is that where we are, have we come to a green plain, with geese, blue streams....? It won't turn out like that, what you hope.'

'Perhaps it's so, what you say – of course, you can't be squeamish if you live upon this globe,' says Sylvain. 'You're right: I'm a collector. What people say, what they do, it all goes on the account, beside the inventory of toys and poisons, it's quite fascinating. But – I'll go down, into the big mixer, just like you. What we have in common, Sabine, is our love of destiny.... Following it along, the way things will turn out... Falling, end over end. Then too – your pigs.... You read a message on them....'

'Not pity, Sylvain,' says Sabine. 'Sadness. So steadfast in their lives. Looking ahead, in file.'

'Emotions are all joined together, Sabine,' says Sylvain. 'You can't have one without the rest.'

'Have it your way, Sylvain,' says Sabine, watching the monkeys up their trees. 'If that's how you see it.'

'I can't follow you, Sabine,' Sylvain says. 'At all events, you'll have more cash than me, if the animals hold their price.'

'Not here, not anywhere I've been,' says Sabine, punching the wall. 'Not the past, and not the present that I've seen. There's no alternative, I know. You need a lot of cash to make a corner of your own, with all your stuff: you salt yourself and wait your turn.... I can't stand it, I can't bear anywhere.'

'That's wrong, Sabine. Another everything? – it's not available, it never has been. Where they said it was – that was first a lie, and then a fantasy,' says Sylvain.

'I'll make you care what happens to me,' Sabine says. Sylvain realises… – no, really he doesn't, doesn't care. Then, there's the monkeys, what to do with them, he thinks, 'When I've accumulated, I'd think about help, a distribution of cash where there's a cry – but be very very careful when you do it,' he tells her, moving as far from her as possible.

*

Oh no! Here comes a complaining lady, a tall horse, tattoos you couldn't miss, nor ignore....

'I love animals,' says Corinne, sweeping in, squeezing Sylvain offhand, a pat, a stroke. 'But, Sylvain – these ones, they steal and make a noise. I translate it as derision. Not to mention all the crap....'

'You could climb the trees and shake them down,' says Sylvain, rather shortly: 'But you may find you prefer them up above your head.'

'It isn't cash,' Corinne says. 'I spend spend spend – maybe I should invest? But – stuff decays, iron rusts. Unless it's Roman, cement goes to dust; I think it was that awful fishpaste they mixed in, probably with the ground bones of their prisoners of war, gnawed by the beasts for fun, they say. "Sport", perhaps – sounds better than "for fun".'

Sylvain brightens – 'This is the lucky day, Corinne,' he says. 'I've just lost all my cash! No one takes advice – so they won't pay for it. I've just found out, I'm destitute! So, yes, invest, only in immortal things ... poetry, symphonies – even sequoias ... even through me....'

'Hmmm,' says Corinne, 'I'll give another spiral to my thought.... The trouble is, our riches. Where they come from, you don't know. And when they go, you don't know where to look.'

'Perhaps they go back into nature,' Sylvain says. 'Like we all shall.'

'Are you on someone's side, Sylvain?' Corinne asks.

'No, you don't need be now,' says Sylvain. 'Not on anyone's. Every mood's a side... I could even be on yours.'

'That seems a contradiction,' Corinne says. 'I only represent myself.'

'That's the side you must be against,' says Sylvain. 'The only one. Doubt yourself, your brothers. You can be a friend of everyone, of every country, or of some – but ... you must stay clear of certain factions, certain individuals, armed and dangerous. The deed.

Propaganda by the deed – it's terrifying! Temptation. Watch those thoughts – how they creep in! The rest – it's all your flowerbed.'

'And it's a relief, I'm sure,' says Corinne. 'Flowers don't climb trees and throw stuff down.'

'Flowers are the trees,' says Sylvain, realising then how trivial that is. 'In nutshells.'

'I know, I know,' says Corinne. 'I do so want you on my side.'

She's very young. It's easy to say she's beautiful, with no offence....

Friends exotic, forceful; a lively, passé gang, if you don't come up against any one of them – and alas, her nose, when she's a matron, toppling the symmetry ... other parts fail, she's not built to last, Sylvain thinks, though it's not done to say, nor even tell her confidentially.

'I should advise you, Corinne,' Sylvain says, 'I have a need for cash – but, as for sex, my attitude is odd. I don't much like it.'

'I'd have found out anyway. Sort the monkeys,' Corinne says. 'Then we'll see what we can do about your deep frigidity.'

'Yesterday, I'd have thought about some help. Today, the story's different,' says Sylvain. 'My sister – she's gone hard. I'll follow her, it is the only winning way. You should deal with her, not me, Corinne.'

*

Corinne's biker friends cut down the trees. The monkeys occupy the building – anyone would tell you, it's much more comfortable.

There is no food. 'I'll have to think,' says Sabine.

Monkeys learn quick. Music is the food – of necessity, as of love – everyone has seen those monkey bands – Meissen, of course. The *style galant* their inspiration. The vanguard, that's them now. Nothing snide, sarcastic – they are good! The joint's ... aflame! They've gigs all round the world – Sabine's railwayman goes, so does the tobacconist – trad jazz is dead, but keeping those monkeys in some luxury – that is a different tale. Watch the number on your ticket for the concert – you might get a prize. The railwayman's number wins – so, he's rich now, he's always played the combination on his badge. They can be dumped now, cap and badge....

'Oh,' says Sabine, 'if another world docked tomorrow, I'd jump on.'

'It would be a spaceship,' Sylvain says. 'Cramped and smelly. You'd need to learn another language – maybe spoken from another orifice. This place is like all places – a place because it connects with others, quite the same.'

'Beauty, truth,' says Sabine, weary, 'they must be everywhere – or else, perhaps nowhere at all.'

'It doesn't follow,' Sylvain says. 'It doesn't matter. I'm destitute. Sabine, your capital's abusive, it squats. Rent the Colosseum, book in your monkey band, on its tour, we'll go see it. Use our thumbs. Maybe we can stay.... No one wants to live there, so there'll be no hassle if we never leave.'

'Well...' says Sabine, unimpressed. 'That city's the navel of the world – useless when you're born, and central only once....'

'I'll follow on,' says Sylvain, thinking of Corinne – her friends who gather cash without relationships, no begging from relatives. Not the good life, but much fizz and chatter. 'Go, Sabine! Those monkeys – they are on a roll. They're virtuosi – all they lack, is self-criticism.. They're the lucky ones – there's no failures....'

'Oh yes there are,' shouts Sabine. 'What's more, they talk to themselves. They question. Can you reconcile protection with freedom? The cage protects – permits a vivisection. But – you're a martyr! Free to spill everything that's in your brain. Gibber, knap flints, be Euclid. A sacrifice, enclosed and fed. That's protection, conservation. All living's a contradiction, long easy life, but jail for ever! All happy – and stupid, except me! What does it signify; living without sacrifice, without tests, free, hunted and defenceless? Or captivity: long caged existences, so the rest, the troop, can live those free and dangerous lives – and then die outcast and worthless. Sacrifice, martyrdom – a free act that gives protection and closes the debate, right or wrong – it's selfish supreme, and unselfish too. Free, protective, as far as you can go...?'

'Nothing, Sabine,' Sylvain says. 'It means nothing at all. It's our arithmetic, the colour of our rainbow ... nature is us, and nurture too.

'A life on the road, touring – is it freedom, or sacrifice? The rootless jingles they play out – it's not creation, not their culture ... is it even ours?'

'Heavy questions,' Sabine says. 'You can't answer. That's the limit – you've found it, you can't evolve so you can answer them. What's more – you can't play a scale, nor modulate.'

'Follow the band, Sabine,' says Sylvain. 'The world once had ends, now, it doesn't finish, it goes round and round, but one day it *will* have an end....'

*

'Corinne, *princesse de Chine....'* says Sylvain. 'They were brought in, over the long wall, for their strength. Princesses from places no one has heard of.'

'I have these friends,' says Corinne. 'I have to get away – they're strong, but in quite the wrong way. You've seen the world, Sylvain, anyone can tell. I place myself ... under your protection. It gives you lustre.'

It's what everyone waits for, all their life – the invitation Corinne gives. It's terrifying. You're lucky if you're already dead. Long ago, protection was the system. A place for the strong, and for the weak – long ago, protection was the system, now there's just the mafia.

'I can't do anything,' says Sylvain. 'My parents left me nothing, nothing in your line. My sister – we share parents too – she's desperate. She's following the music.

What persecutes you, Corinne? Texaco, Monsanto, France, the customary histories?'

'You can see how I am,' Corinne says, 'I'm creole. It's urgent, what I ask.... Escape, or shelter ... what can you offer?'

'I've had the ambition to be creole,' says Sylvain. 'Hard to accommodate. Choices, Corinne – they multiply, and we diminish thinking of them, knowing we're too old, too unsupple, too plain.... There's Sabine – she thinks the monkeys run her. It's true: they preferred Paris to Rome, they went, she had to follow – she's a scientist, the object takes you over, you peer into the cage, the screen – all becomes a puzzle, one-dimensional. Instead of your inside, your circle, your perceptions – it's all a mystery, a secret to solve – outside, not you. You're a detective – never the judge, never can you do a crime or shoot a suspect ... usually you find there is no crime at all....'

'You're trying to evade me?' Corinne asks. 'I hear those monkeys make a rousing sound....'

'At least it's improvised,' Sylvain says. 'The genres shift. First it was free jazz, then they made a tape, it's electronic, then they breathed, and it was jungle. People go to anything if the tickets are hard to find, and there's a lottery.'

'Help me, Sylvain,' Corinne says.

'Our fathers let us down, Corinne,' Sylvain says. 'They were bog lights, they helped, they shimmered, they were immersed. We tried, Sabine and I, our two fathers showed us paths we couldn't take. My advice, analyses, it went in with all the rest, and finished bad... Help? Everybody needs it, more and more....'

'I'm with the monkeys,' says Corinne. 'They're right. What's more – Paris every time.'

'Yes,' says Sylvain. 'But they don't know they're right.'

'They don't care,' says Corinne. 'And they use their resource better than you do, Sylvain. They explore, and if what they find does not excite – then, they don't care. That's good. I care, though. I care about me. Help!'

'The music that they do,' says Sylvain, 'It makes good sense to us – but them ... they are not of our world, of our collective mind. They don't communicate with us – the music's like the nuptial parlour of the bower birds, patterns of geese up high, crows' jewellery.... What we appreciate is not what birds make for themselves.... It's how it fits what *we* have made.'

'Yes, yes,' says Corinne, 'that's what the whitecoats say. But – you never heard the talking drums, Sylvain, and nor did I. Those speak direct, if you could hear them. Besides, these works, after a while, their makers, their society, what they say is ours – all die. Ageing, the works seem familiar, though they ought to be more alien. The Cyclades speak clearer than the Parthenon.... Beneath all this, Sylvain, there is a lie – our society, it does not belong to us. We're in it, that is all. The music – belongs to no one, it's not the evidence that there's a universal society that is ours. We shall discuss all this – it never ends. But I have needs, an urgency....'

'Of course,' says Sylvain, 'of course, there is communication. The music isn't bad, but who am I to say – I cannot play a scale or modulate....'

Corinne says, 'See – I'm armed.'

'Being a creole,' Sylvain repeats, 'has always fascinated me – a thing I wanted, couldn't have. Not ever. For me, it is a terminus.'

'I can protect you, Sylvain,' Corinne says, 'from what you'll never have. Do this for me – protect me from my friends....!'

'Here, there's just the good and the bad, Corinne,' Sylvain says. 'Could it be, you're still in with the bad? Even though you broke the rules? People here think every rule is good....'

'We could move, Sylvain,' says Corinne. 'Those other places, they are full of everything. From a distance it's a scene, but close to, we won't have good and bad, just rules you keep or move around. In every street and dwelling, there's a different set of them, like pizza dough, they end up round but all are thick or thin: today, tomorrow ... it rains, it snows – what could be more different?'

'It sounds hard,' says Sylvain. 'Harder than here – except, our rules for robots: those, we have to keep. For us, who're neither good nor bad, keeping the path is just as difficult. Hold things together – people, "friends" – hi town lo town – need a funicular. Help? Don't imagine it, your mafia, Corinne; help's the last thing they will give.... You need to know what makes each, and other people, stick together.'

'Yes,' says Corinne, 'but that's not it. Rules are one thing: good, bad, that's quite another. It would be difficult to be all good, all bad, if that was what you want. I never met a person who....'

'Oh, no doubt there are,' says Sylvain, seeing in Corinne's bid for his protection, death.

'Well,' he asks, 'aren't you going to tell me stories? About your home? The priests, the murders, the awful ends, the lucky breaks with animals – making you a fortune or offering a magic ride? Everybody tells....'

'That's why I shan't,' says Corinne. 'Remember this,' and she shows him her persuader – it's like a fruitknife, a butterknife with the round end broken and filed into a point. 'It works best on a naked skin,' she says. 'But of course, it means you've to get close up, and in a special circumstance.'

'No family tales, then?' asks Sylvain. 'No saga?'

'Sagas have fathers,' says Corinne, 'though not so many fathers as you have. Epics are for orphans. That's me.'

'I'm having a silly kind of life,' says Sylvain. 'Better to say – a stupid kind. You could be my big thing, Corinne – or more of the same. It's all in the origins, don't you think? But then – everybody's origins are the same. Narrow the focus – and it all depends on sides, which ones you can choose, which hunt you down. You can call it chance, to dodge the substance. But it's sides, Corinne...'

'I was the lucky child,' Corinne says. 'My father was corrupt. He took money – they called him a public servant, but really, he was a private boss. That way, you grow up knowing everything and everyone. They all come, deferential, showing their best side, and you can treat them exactly as you want: then watch.'

'My father was a drunk,' says Sylvain. 'His clients were the drunks. He made the drunk ones drunker, some so drunk they gave up drink: they had the intoxication permanent, within. Then he wanted to help another way, and disappeared. I was lucky too – I saw them all, unfettered, kicking high.'

'It doesn't matter,' says Corinne. 'Why should it? You find out about yourself, or not – what's the consequence?'

'Why select me?' Sylvain asks. 'If you really want escape – do it on your own. Don't trust other people.'

'You know about wars and backhanders, and deal with people who pay you for writing it all down – but you gain nothing for yourself. You've no interests, except obedience,' Corinne says. 'Finishing the job, showing them what they can do. I trust you, you're naive.'

'Your father will have left you enemies,' says Sylvain.

'That's why you need dangerous friends,' says Corinne. 'When there's cadavers, it's too late – the cops, at mealtimes, they don't answer phones....'

'I'm not sure this is my thing,' Sylvain says. 'It smells like sacrifice.' He doesn't mention Bernie – who'd remember anyway?

'We find poor defenceless people,' Corinne says. 'Defend them. Then, when the enemy comes – we all fight to protect our rights. You think it's selfish, Sylvain? It's what lions and great apes do.... If only some bad guys had not given it all a downward spin....'

*

The long grey walls are like a cloud, laid on grey-yellow hills. Far inside, you see a town: ochre – mud or sandstone; the vegetation's sparse, so you'd think it's mud.... It's motionless.

'This is it,' Corinne says. 'This is where I'm needed.'

'I'll see you settled,' Sylvain says. And then....

'Why move on? I have a creed,' Sylvain thinks. 'That does well here. Protect the weak, bring happiness to the animals' short lives, store up the unread books, don't mutilate the women. I could stay, sell things. Be wise. Leave.'

'Naturally, there's rebels,' says Corinne. 'What do you expect? There's not much here but rigour, dissent and history. No one is interested in us.'

Everybody's interested, naturally – but Corinne's right. No one knows her, her past, or why she's here, and what she'd bring.

'Stay with me, Sylvain,' says Corinne. 'You won't see Sabine again – she's famous now. Besides – she stole those monkeys, they weren't hers, they're someone else's capital. She'll go to jail, and worse for them. She doesn't think of you, remember you. Her heart, her instinct – her obsession – it's brought her down. She is a troubled soul, Sylvain. Now: look at me – if you knew true love, you'd stay... It'd be the nearest thing to being creole...'

'But I don't feel true love, Corinne,' says Sylvain, wondering how he'll leave.

'Not "feel", Sylvain,' she says: '"Know". Oppression – the soldiers fight, they man the walls, they fall back into cellars, traps and suicides. They don't feel oppression – but they know about it, that's what they have to fight. That's what they are. I know we ask, we ask continually – what are they, Sylvain, all those soldiers? Are they oppression or its contrary? That question doesn't occur, mostly, to normal people. It doesn't matter. First, whichever side they're on, the soldiers know they have to win. It's the same with love, Sylvain: someone wins, someone has to lose. If you lose, and you survive, there's a camp, then they bus you somewhere, and you start again.'

'I'm not ready for a picture that's that big,' says Sylvain.

*

People are suspicious here – some with a smile, and some with a shutting of the door. They're right – Corinne's an angel, but suspicious people up above, outside – they turn uneasy when she's near.

There's a playground, rusted through. Sylvain plays – it's right, he won't have kids, it's up to him. The swings you need a relative to make them work, the ropes have gone. The round thing – to make it work you need some loyal friends, who make it whirl, don't push you off. There's bars to show you're strong. And there's a chute. You have to use the chute to come to earth, the ladder's dangerous, so down the twisty snake you go – too late, you see the level part has gone – you hit the dusty soil, and down you go, and keep on down, like the dark web except it is dimensional – there's galleries that run away, and men with picks and jewels set shining in their heads, who prise off slabs of opal, jade, chalcedony – but on you go, the colours go from red and yellow to a grim green, purple and grey, the gods go from amber to dark blue, they've skulls around their belts, tiaras shining with your neighbour's eyes plucked by those crones astride the piles of smoked brown corpses dumb as logs ... and down you go, past thrones and equerries – all look surprised, but no one tries to slow you down, and there's a stink of putputs, motor tricycles piled high with muslins and there's kids who steal whatever falls off the carts, and oh the bundles, there's guys who gather up the horse shit, sort the whole grains, hermits and heretics, and there's preachers too with scrolls of careful writing made in ostrich shapes and sounding out like wooden trumpets, metres long, recruiters everywhere, those guns are beautiful, the stocks of pearl and brass, you get a tall cloth hat, a little lacquer box to keep your powder in, and prostitutes, so beautiful you know you can't afford, the boys – they offer everything, but down you go, and there are pelts of everything – the black cows' and the human ones, and stuff that's used until it's dead and will not resurrect – and you don't hit, although you've seen it all, and been through empires and their occupations, slogged it out on snowy roads and sand that gets inside your prick. And that's how it's been here, you too, and everywhere, except you look up in the light and see that almost all the houses have been knocked down now and heaved back partly up. The silence: and you know they've hunted down the animals, you have no sister here, nothing passed on, no story and no primal thirst – and as you've travelled down, your memory expands, like an anenome, a paper flower dropped into raki, the arms that clutch indiscriminate with the tide, puce, purple, pink, and rust, you know it all, you lie upon the ground – and you are angry –

'I was here to help, Sylvain,' says Corinne. 'All people in the town. Not food, but information.... Now, there's just a part I want to organise, make them ready for the fight.... Only a part – that's why there's silence here....'

'Who against who?' asks Sylvain. 'Who whom?'

'Without me, Sylvain,' Corinne says, 'you'll have to organise. You know exactly who is who, you have to organise your side, and shoot the spies, and give protection to the kids, give them guns, if you can trust them, put a sign on all the houses of the other side.'

'It's absolutely alien to me,' Sylvain says. 'Corinne! I made a picture of all this, I sold it on, spheres of influence, balances of power, all that, but I'm not part...'

'You know exactly what's what,' Corinne repeats. 'If you don't – now's your chance. You can redress any wrong. Stop being silly, even stop being stupid. Do your best – that's what morality is for. When you're finished, hand it on. Don't faddle life away, not like Sabine!'

'This place,' says Sylvain. 'I don't belong...'

'You've said it many times,' says Corinne. 'It's like all other places. And it's in your blood – taking a lead.'

'It's unforgivable improvisation...' Sylvain says. 'It would be...'

'Reflect, Sylvain,' Corinne says. 'Forgiving won't occur for anyone. Improvising – it always takes place on a ground, with rules and techniques, expectations, audience – all there. That's been your best preparation yet.... Everybody says it's good and bad – not blurs and pastels, fudges and riddles, taradiddles – that everybody recognises now. There's no escape, Sylvain: follow the right, the good....'

'It's intricate, Corinne,' says Sylvain, almost pleading. 'I'm not in control of all the detail. I don't feel worthy of a trust, still less the master...'

'Well, now it's what you are,' she says. 'I leave you here, that is your task – remember, as commander, you must think of following an order: first, raise morale! A dance, a singsong, then be sure you've a clear line you can retreat along, that supplies will reach you, that your scouts are told the passwords, that when the mortars pin you down you have a strategy, a sense napoleonic of why you're there and how you'll win. You are their hope, Sylvain. Identify your side, deal with the rest as everybody does... So what you know is right, whatever it may cost.'

There isn't much Sylvain can say.

'If you're creole,' says Corinne. 'This is your gift. This is what the species needs, this is your mission, and you know, just as you said – it was your ambition too, to be creole, to stop your indeterminacy, your nothingness, your dither, dull black-and-whiteness. Take control, do the right thing, and – be like me.'

3

LALIX, ACHILLE & DOMINIC

'MOTHER WILL TELL you what to do!' says Lalix 'She's brilliant. That guy Sylvain – who didn't last so long, he started it, then someone much more suitable sprang up and took it on. If she takes you on, and it kills you, well, it's part of life, and she has given you your turn. She sees a sequence – not what disaster may be on the cards, but how to punch out a theme – weak follows strong, the red the black, the brutal follows vain – she sees the ordinary grey as it is formed, and she is right: the best there is or can be, it comes out through the interludes of negative, the shaky positives – like monkeys holding on their elders' tails, prancing bright and vigorous.'

'My father was a patient of his father,' says Achille. 'Split personality, I think.'

'Another beauty and the beast?' and Lalix laughs. 'The zoos are packed with them. To Corinne, you mustn't say your life is disappointing – she'll find a challenge for you that will strip your flesh. We have to move around – some of her friends are criminals, and others are good people she's dropped in the sea – if they survive the sharks, the predators go after her.... The criminals – they fix things, they emote, they justify themselves. Good guys are bewildered, you love them because nothing they want is ever done.'

*

'Yes,' says Lalix, 'we're all creoles here. Can't you tell, how my mother says pah*dì* as pah*dà*? We creoles shall inherit the earth, it's written down.'

'I didn't know that,' Achille says, 'I never heard Corinne talk that way.'

There's a peaceful moment.

'I need to make a point with you, Lalix,' Achille says. 'When we're out together, you go off with someone else, and come back only when I take you home.'

'I can't stand jealousy, Achille,' she says.

'It's not that, Lalix. It's that you're somewhere else, another world. Not a reality we share,' Achille says.

'I can't stand scenes,' she says.

'Don't cry, Lalix,' Achille says. 'Look, I'm crying too....'

'I can't stand people crying,' Lalix says, crying more. 'We can compromise.... I love you so, Achille....'

'No,' Achille says, 'you have to change, Lalix.

'Look, Achille,' Lalix says. 'Shape up. Get a grip. We can give you a hard, a very hard, experience. Don't fuck with us – we have resources....'

'I'm having one now already,' says Achille. 'A hard time, a bad experience.'

*

'What can they do? Break your legs?' asks Dominic, Achille's friend. 'That's not a cure for sex.'

'The family,' says Achille. 'It's unpredictable. Charities, insurrections – they use you in their causes. They need your loyalty – absolutely, until the end. It's dark, what they do, they rely on people from the shadow side: slithery guys, who tell on you.'

He pulls a face – a wounded swain, lovesick, they say. 'We're all creoles,' Achille says, 'We shan't inherit anything.'

'Listen,' says Dominic, tiring of Achille's love stories – 'Heaven and earth – if you don't believe in Heaven, you can't believe in Earth. Its solidity, its permanence. Its plenitude of shadows, metaphors, its double sense. You can't believe in what you do not know. Nor in cats, spectres – the mysteries... Good mysteries, bad mysteries, not just mysterious mysteries – you must demystify all that. What we must understand is the universe – but which? The infinity of failed universes, gibbers of particles, neutron soup gone coursing down the cracks, rejected, dissipated.... Just one by chance seems sticky solid, materialises... this briefly bears us up.'

'Is "infinity" the right word, Dominic?' Achille asks. '"Trials", maybe. I agree about the mysteries. Probably they aren't, but for a time they were described as that.... Remember Sufis?.... They were mysterious till the tourists came. Now, here you go, inventing more, specialised, cosmic uncertainties. The ineffable, you'd say ... needing a universal scale. A first cause is denied, another one more perfect's postulated, practising its trial and error ... finally gelling stones and dust to make the porridge that we're standing on.'

'Think it over,' Dominic says. 'You'll see I'm right. Or wrong. We're all human, different each one, so of course each has a slant, a spin, that could take in everything, if we so wish, and find the puzzle in it still. Take colonies: everyone knows why they're created; the money and the power, the arms and legs, the faithful and the cannon fodder. Lalix colonised you – but she neglects you, she's absent-minded. So – you want to colonise *her*. It's common.'

'Colonies ... think of the overlays, the rulers and the cultures, put into new colours – think! – the Deccan.... We're always being colonised, Dominic,' Achille says. 'It never stops, and the past – it doesn't wash away.'

'Is Corinne the empress? Is there an empire now? Is it dead, or is it everywhere? For sure it's not Lalix or you,' says Dominic.

'You're a poet, Dominic,' says Achille. 'That must be why I can't follow you. If you don't believe in Earth, you stop believing in Hell as well. I wonder – how can you stop? I'm earthbound, but where am I...? What is underneath: up there? Is there an up, a down?'

'Everything can be explained – that's what languages are for,' says Dominic. 'You must fit. You belong somewhere, so you must be loved.'

'I'm not a colony,' says Achille. 'I don't believe in empire. Or Corinne. Where does that leave me? What must I believe in? And suppose I don't...'

'Oh, I do,' says Domonic cheerfully. 'Believe. Everybody does. Tattered stuff. Does this help with Lalix, Achille?'

'Maybe with Lalix,' Achille says, his tears long forgotten. 'My faith in her has gone. But some belief remains, it's true, in who is hunting me.'

It's stasis.

'I need help, Dominic,' Achille says. 'And – I loved Lalix so.... But – no mystery. No puzzle ... maybe the cosmos gives us one, too big to handle.... Everything was shaky, now it's dangerous too.'

'Forget that,' says Dominic. 'There's no small mysteries, true. The large ones you won't penetrate. Deal with Lalix. Prepare to leave Corinne's realm ... then, leave the empire. Is it possible? I'm sure you'll find out. It doesn't bother me, but be sure – I'm on your side.'

*

'It's the tension, Dominic,' Achille says. 'Corinne wants Lalix and me to work together, go back a hundred years, some ancient place. It's because we two are severed – she knows we'll watch each other close, defer, harass, shout, scream and weep. Those are the principles of vigorous governance. She won't spare me, or Lalix....'

'Calm, Achille,' says Dominic. 'You're protected everywhere! She can't fire you. Lalix, is she the only daughter? Is she expendable...?'

'I don't want protection, Dominic,' Achille says. 'It's not my thing, though – being a satrap, a chancellor. I'm not a warrior – I may want to paint. Grow stuff with trumpets on the end. Bind wounds, distribute wealth....'

'You can't,' says Dominic. 'That's what I do – but I'm a success.... Yours would be wilfulness....'

'No,' Achille says: 'Not will – insight. The machines, the falling rate of profit, value vanified – it all manufactures free time, time that is empty, dull duration. All that's left to fill the void is vapid work, precarious, mechanical, low-paid... Security and soldiers. They call it "no work". Really, we must welcome, re-elaborate "no-work" – it's the alternative, the "post", where activity will be joyful and productive....'

'You'll find,' says Dominic, 'that crises are resolved. Free time is not the system's end – the system loves a crisis, overcoming them is its gymnastics. After the crisis, you wouldn't be a wage-slave, but you'd join the beggar's union, run a stall that sells old shoes.... And, you know, Lalix says fierce things, but underneath, she's tender. A long-pig, cooked in a pit, wrapped in soft leaves ... so tempting, and enough for all.'

'Corinne,' says Achille, more tears hustling close, 'Shapes us all. She finds a place that's desperate. Silent too. People need help: of course, you must provide, you think. But some face more than poverty or droughts: hostility, ostracism – enough to push them out. They try to live on, isolated, sabotaged. They have to ask for help. They want to stay, for if they move they'll need more help, be destitute, where they were only persecuted. Only a part's involved – a sect, a dialect, a trade, a book, a name. There's always some, only a part too, who persecute. Then, there's people with some cash, some protection, a handle on the market, people with cover; quiet among the bigots, the blusterers, there's the timid, the indifferent. There's victims, bullies, and the in-between. *There* is the crisis, Dominic. The middle, moderates – *there's* the flaw.

'Corinne organises both the help, and the resistance. *You* have to help, Dominic. *They* have to fight, resist. And so – it's up to you to organise the fight. Corinne is the benefactor, the warrior queen: and she controls. She has the power.... It isn't about her – she gives the means to carry on.'

'All the parcels ... the guns ... the countries, and the conferences,' says Dominic. 'It's unimaginable, although you've seen it many times.'

'It's what she does,' says Achille. 'Heavy things; transforming everything. There's nothing more for you to do. It's family.'

'Achille,' says Dominic, 'your naiveté appals. You're not holy, but fool's a career still open for you. What you describe – the selfless and the armed – it's so banal. Knowledge must be common – this is trite.... Everybody knows already what you've just discovered...'

He lights up – an electric pipe, bosky smoke with hints of weed. 'I was sensitive,' he says. 'So, I was sent to military school. You have to run and run – my tendon snapped... If it was yours, Achille – how they'd have laughed!... You have to live in different spheres – in one you suffer, in the other laze on lotus pads.'

'China!' Achille says. 'They won't let Corinne in! They will resist – there is the party, Lenin's party, and a plan for fifty years ... all kinds of phases, on to socialism, equality, all that....'

'It's all a dream,' says Dominic. 'We'll be gone in fifty years; all of us – even the flying bugs... It's true, they won't let Corinne in. It doesn't help you, you and Lalix...'

*

'Achille is a child,' says Lalix. 'I wanted one, till it was him. Now – it's a bore.'

'He has no grasp,' says Dominic. 'The weakness – it comes from father's strength. A flaw, passed down, a reticence – it always magnifies, it's a blot, grease spot. What absorbs, carries and colours what is vulnerable. The fault becomes immense, the statue weeps and bleeds, the hero fails the test, is locked back in his block of ice. The mountain closes on the soldier, her faithful horse runs off....'

'That's apposite,' says Lalix, sizing him up. 'I need a horse. A racing saddle – it's so light.... You could try it out, my dear....'

Dominic flexes his hocks – 'I know where I'm going, Lalix – that's one better than a horse!'

'You're so receptive, Dominic,' says Lalix. 'You've done well – even from what they call effeminate things: writing, drawings, little plans you don't know which way they're up.'

'That's how work is now, Lalix,' says Dominic. 'Fiddle and pry, copy and steal,' he laughs.

'Poor Achille – he just mooned around,' says Lalix. 'Waiting for his day.'

'He's my friend,' says Dominic, 'so I won't do him down. He cries a lot, it's true.'

'Corinne, of course – she never wastes a thing,' says Lalix, making her bra more comfortable.

'This chant of 'some there be without a tombstone' – she won't sing along. 'To every stiff, his or her memorial.' She's strict on that. No anonimity, no dust to dust, everybody has their use, their usefulness. Even in death. Burn us up, make us smog – what reverence lies in that?' she asks.

'Well, speaking of Achille – he's always seemed immortal – approaching it, at least,' says Dominic. 'In life – his use is not so clear. What will death and after bring, I wonder, Lalix?'

'Oh yes, I wonder too,' she says. 'And, Dominic – I love to talk with you – the last things, that's their name. It makes me go all goosey. When I think what is to come.... Of course, the angels work it out – they double check, take things into due account: it's all done thoroughly, I'm sure.'

'Once we know that it will come, it doesn't matter much exactly how, or when – we're here for little time, and there are big things we must set upright,' says Dominic. 'Those of us who see, those who can act – there's no time to lose in hanging round.'

'Tributes to give, a score or two to settle...' says Lalix. 'Don't ask me to take reprisals against Achille – I know I sound off. He was oppressive, disrespectful. Of my mother too. I'd like to rehab him, make a use for him. There's many places where he'd have a role, be a symbol, even totemic. Have his day....'

'Forget him, Lalix,' Dominic says. 'There's so much we could do together....'

'Yes!' says Lalix. 'Losing weight is one... You need a partner, Dominic,' and she pinches rolls of flesh, lifting her top to show.... 'But you're not one to believe in love,' and she laughs.

'One mustn't rush,' says Dominic. 'You never know. Love! – that's something that may never happen – no angels keeping score! Or it falls on you, like a tile drops off a roof....'

'It's a project, Dominic,' says Lalix. 'You must always have them – lots.'

'Oh, I have lots,' says Dominic. 'A musical, movies. A TV chain ... but you'll find they cost.'

'We feel you need to take a side,' says Lalix. 'Not just prance on stage. Everyone. Most things are near their points of non-return. Nothing will be like it is, nothing that is, is like it was – that's evident. So – take a side. Invent and fight ... join in the whirl.'

'Who does your mother hope will win?' asks Dominic. 'The struggle she promotes – which side? I'm curious.'

'Oh,' says Lalix. 'You don't know. Not till it's over. Justice isn't bringing down the axe, you know – it's all a process. It takes years, or centuries – those present at the start, for sure they'll age and creak. It's like an opera – you love, you die – but at the end you all come on, alive and dead, collect applause and measured recognitions – people who've never been seen on stage at the same time. They've fought, they had their principles, there's a division – but, the plot has brought them all together. In the end – there they all are, every element and alloy, electrum and brass, the resurrected, the quick, the dead, enslaved or armed – even the voice coach and the prompt.'

'Those shows I've planned – they're orderly, the most order I allow myself,' says Dominic.

'That's fascinating,' Lalix says. 'I was going to tell you – that pipe! You in the smoke! Delphic! Being hooked – it's the most ordered thing. You're an addict, obviously – but what to?'

'Oh,' says Dominic, 'I try – but nothing climbs aboard. No monkey on my back, no golden arm to cuddle it, no tic, nothing I can't do without. No smoke, sometimes the fire, Lalix....'

'I knew it!' Lalix shouts. 'You're a Brassens. A Neinsager, a bad boy. I love it! You've not surrendered, you contest! That's your needle!'

*

'Dear Dominic,' Corinne exclaims. 'I see you in the family. Let's put Achille in the box – up to the attic with him. He was for kiddies – he never took a side, said that was vieux chapeau.... We'll show him, Lalix. Put him out of sight....'

That's what they do. It doesn't hurt – that part at least. He had this weakness: – love betrayed him ... maybe it was love he failed...

*

The African doesn't speak – if he'd been selling figurines or masks, Achille would have bought. Instead, he gives the guy a coin. 'This,' he says weightily, 'for the English who made you a country impossible to live in, and gave you nothing – for the Americans who took your resources, the French whose army overran your northern provinces. You ought to hate them all, like I do, for the past, for blocking off the future....'

'Yes,' says the guy, 'thanks,' and leaves. He's very cheerful. The days are dull, but not so bad, it seems. The coin is less than you would tip a slave – but he's done nothing, after all, to merit it.

'No melancholy, no irony, no moralism, no regrets,' Achille thinks. 'What's gone and done – goodbye! I've sewn my stomach up, I live in a real robotic future – that's how I save money to collect – monochromes, especially black, not the gaudy stuff.'

Nowhere to put them, but – this is a rich place, this is what you do – collect: even if you have to fight as well, or suffer assaults and fanfares in the street.

It's all there. Nothing is there. The connections are all in a future place, where you'll make sense of everything – 'I've just been,' Achille thinks. 'I've had all my history, my representation. In a rough crowd ... a holy scrum ... a self-portrait ... in a mirror ... in a still-life on a table ... in my son's body ... in my corpse. This is as good as it will come, and I'm as happy as I'll ever be.

'I'm walking down the street, the street is walking down me. My brain is soldered in a can, the can is in the trash – it's compacted, it's going round and round, it connects over and under with everyone who sees it – thousands of those cans, millions, all coming to an end, quick, quick – there's a shrill sound as a can enters the compactor, and it's finished ... you never know more – it's finished. The metal's flattened out again – but something will remain, have been learned.... What? The compactor only takes the highest value coin there is – before there's another journey, windborne, fluttering like a cloud, up your bets and stake! The famous guys they have another slot – the paper! with the hologram, the currency you've learned to trust ... there's not much time to spend it and be obsolete. This will be the last, the decisive battle, for everyone. Then comes the call – "save the princess, load your gun..."'

*

Everybody's waiting, waiting for that call, apotheosis, or perhaps just punishment. Achille talks over with his friend Cécile – how things went bad with Lalix... While he talks, he sees Cécile's become attentive, quivering a bit –

'After all,' says Cécile, 'Corinne, her gang – aren't insects. The old ones don't kill and eat discarded suitors, don't defend their little plump defenceless ones with suicidal stings.... They've bigger things.... Besides, you've got protection, Achille – they'll never get you...'

'We must be insects,' says Achille, holding her as she twists, tries to dance, maybe – 'We two. The bugs know what survival means, and what they have to do – we live a day, and we must make a million eggs – oh no! down they go! A carp! He'll see off a million kids, a mouthful ... hurry Cécile.... I'm ready now, I'm hot.... On with the urge! We're bugs!'

'Yes, Achille, that's how it will be, must be – you have to hurry up,' Cécile says, rearing and ramping up – 'I'm on heat once in a lifetime, this is your day, and mine! – we're turtles mating – the position's mysterious ... or hermaphrodites, snails with our pricks poking out our ears.... Then there's the names, everybody needs one – all those offspring, struggling in the sand, one in a thousand may survive ... what name, Achille?' she asks, ogling, vamping.... 'Shall we give?'

'Oh, give her a pseudonym, Cécile, an anonym,' he says. 'Or else – call her a princess. See, everybody knows me, my long story, my tale – who was I, Cécile? What brought me down? Sex? Who shall I have been? Dying after a profusion of infertility? Not performing: that was my fault! Carried bleeding off the stage!'

Achille's still flaming, but Cécile says, 'Oh no – you're spoiling it! The passion's gone, the sand's run out, I come on heat in forty years, long after I have died...'

'Yes,' Achille says, 'the urge has passed. The words were plentiful, and fired me up – but, ah! my poor flesh! It doesn't follow discourse: those insects, living for a screw, and then quite cheerful, they accept the consequence – the penis broken off, the loved one eats you ... you're pregnant with a thousand pustules, die when they are born.... No, Cécile – the stimulus was there, but those are little monsters, those consequences: – our reason defeats our impulses....'

'Well, stout Achille,' Cécile says. 'What now? Aid, service, or the fight?'

'Service before everything, of course,' Achille says. 'But – when war comes – they send a postcard, a reminder....'

Lalix and Dominic – they don't send a thing. If it's your time is up – you know it, in the instant... Your weak spot ... painted on, it throbs. Lalix told you – don't fuck with them.

*

Money. That's how Corinne manages. You back your side. Charity takes its form, sometimes it's food, sometimes it's guns. Sometimes your side wins, and sometimes not – but your side is always right. It's obvious, that's why it's yours. Money – it runs over baked earth until it finds a crack, and then it disappears – beneath the earth, there's a huge stack of it – the water, the old gods laid it down, and now – the falling rate of profit nothwithstanding – we drink it down, pour it on our heads, anoint ourselves, some bloat and others dessicate, but my! it's necessary, and it's useful.... Nations and splinters, sects and universals – it fires you up, one or more of these inspires you when you're young, you grow, the world changes with you.... You've drunk your ration. The water's gone. You want a soft landing, if a smooth take-off was your dream. The earth is yours; the limitless sky, what's left, is someone else's.

'War, Corinne, bad weather,' Achille says. 'But for those, we'd live modest occluded lives. Wars cleanly won, of course....'

'No!' says Cécile. 'You'd always be soft, a quietist. You can't just wait over and over for the strongest side to win. Corinne is muscle. She does running on the spot, she trains. You, Achille, you need to satisfy someone in your life, or you're a phantom limb, looking for a body to stick on. Lalix is right – you must get out there, cause pain, tell everyone you're right.'

Poor Achille, poor Cécile – even with the love goddess by his side, propping up his spear – he falters.... Cècile is angry – who knows why, but that's the way it is. If Achille had a shield, he'd be taken off on it, maybe buried on it – a stagbeetle upcast....

*

'Oh Corinne,' says Lalix. 'Don't you tire of it? The men, the Achille and the Dominic ... the disasters ... the hungry victims and the pumped-up shifty fanatics, all your "help and sacrifice" ... the repetition that you bring, the iteration that you serve...? The states, the repression, the resistance ... the circle never ending, never broken, the new disasters, the new poverty.... How can you keep on, chasing your tail and everybody else's?'

'Oh Lalix,' Corinne says. 'Everybody thinks that. Then they think – "It will all end soon, very soon.... I'll leave my print in the rock, lay out my monochromes like fossil skeletons, those fiddly ferns in copperplate, the whole collection." Always, it gets broken up, things you'd think eternal, they seem to crumble. Settlements abandoned, castles dissolved....'

'Everybody knows that, Corinne,' Lalix says, 'but you have to do it. If you must submit to history, you have to crawl along, slow ... slow and stupid....'

'Exactly, Lalix,' Corinne says. 'There's nothing else. Trial and error – that is science.'

'The renegade Engels, the evolutionary?' says Lalix. 'Enough of that! Ending as replicants – what a flop!

Dominic the blowhard, Achille the precious, the protected mollusc on his perch – enough!'

'I don't aspire to revolution, Lalix,' Corinne says, 'I drive it all along, the world, its history.'

'You're not all bad,' says Lalix. 'Parts of you are excellent.'

'Justice, mangoes, tapwater, equality, justice,' says Corinne. 'You'll find those go together. It takes time. And who said good or bad, Lalix? It's all a mix. Besides, you'd be the last to know how to differentiate....'

'I can't wait for all that,' says Lalix. 'One step forward, two steps back....'

'To fire a gun, you have to eat. To eat – you have to fire a gun. Then there's the noncombats: who stole their food? Built those dams, bought motorcars? Clubbed them with a modernity? It was voting ruined them, Lalix: they thought they wouldn't need to fight. Voting and TV: vipers with a siren's voice. I bring suffering, Lalix, I know. It's good.'

'I know,' says Lalix. 'It's science – trial and error.'

'Sometimes you puff like Dominic,' Corinne says: 'And you've weak spots like Achille. You could end real bad – not in the moral sense, but smashed up in the alleyway.'

'I don't see who can stop me, strike me down,' says Lalix.

'You're sure, Lalix?' asks Corinne. 'No deal? You could be the angel, bringing the stuff, handing it out. Achille or Dominic – they'd do the politics. Organising the fight: diplomacy, gun-running, cash.'

'They're so incongruous...' Lalix says: 'And Dominic – he smells.'

'You're not immortal, Lalix,' Corinne says. 'The trade is dangerous. It isn't that it leads somewhere you would recognise... You wander on your own – but look at all those camel bones around! Ships of the desert, never making port.'

'I shan't die,' says Lalix. 'I'm not immortal, I'm a black bird. They all look the same, and I shall see you buried, all of you, every one.'

'Brave talk,' says Corinne. 'Remember Sabine – she wanted to conduct, went in the cage, and started to wave her arms. The musicians, those big nimble apes ... a conductor's always an insult, a provocation. That was the last chord for her....'

'I have the law beside me,' Lalix says. 'It sleeps, a sheathèd sword.'

'Exactly so,' says Corinne. 'What luck, to have been colonised by Bonaparte, and then the Duce – we have a law without a right or wrong, a good or bad – the death of all involved does not give pause to justice and its onward march.... Be the agent, Lalix, never the victim be.... and remember the song – "learning to live – it is too late already". Ah those French chansons! – the *feuilles d'autonne* sprouting on every branch...'

'No more splinters for me,' says Lalix, ignoring her. 'No separatisms, only universals. Those obscure movements, Corinne – little states born in silence, suppressed with squeals – bourgeois nationalisms, mother! Mine's the big game – arise! Forget the wretchedness – it isn't real, it's not a starting point... Better stand that Xi-thought on its head – back from slave societies to military democracy... Besides – when they assess my ahievements, all these terms will be forgot....'

'Take care, Lalix,' Corinne says. 'You may be forgot as well. Scavengers – that's what awaits. Knowing metals and recovering them – that's the art, boiling old bones for soup.... It's what Aragon said, 'there is no happy love' – we loved being part of the species, and then everybody let everybody down.'

'Amazons,' says Lalix, indifferent to warnings. 'Communist Amazons. Dominic would not have fit.'

'He aspired to be a mogul,' says Corinne: 'He didn't want to fit. But don't exaggerate, Lalix – of course Amazons are communists. Primitive too. Like Jenny the Pirate. But here's a thing – you may call me mother – but I'm not. I gave you everything, but not your birth.'

'Well, anyway,' says Lalix, anxious to be off, recruit her Amazons. 'We're all still creoles, mother. Birth comes as an imperative, not a gift – a gift can be recycled, babies can't.'

'Oh yes they can, that's what I told you,' Corinne said. 'When you tire of Amazons – you can seek out your origin, your Firmine. Make a movie of your quest.... Behind us, Lalix, there's a yearning for excess, I'm sure: addicted ancestors. Leaving us rummaging to find our inner aeroplane. The thing to do – is make it happen outside, outside yourself. Only the quite normal ones can paint the town and put in monster statues by the pond. If you're altered, it's all staged inside – the colours and the bronze. Your brain – it smelts, it throws acrylic at the walls.

'Families, you know – they must go on, and on. I found them – stones round your neck, but not to make you drown – Achille, Dominic – they were to give you weight. I know how it all works, you see, but still I try, I hope – and I repeat, over and over, fail, renounce – and fall again. Multiply. That's the order of the day, and every day. You, Lalix, lack that sense of movement.... I, we, wake, feel bad, but must repeat the day ... in detail, touching every corner just so many times....'

'Oh, I'm more capable than you think,' says Lalix, starting down the path that leads to Amazonia: 'the Black Sea, the Maghreb, Brazil – each a cradle of the Amazons, all creole in their ways. There is a choice – steppe, jungle, desert .... each can breed my destiny...'

'Don't mess with myth,' Corinne shouts. 'It's true they took precautions, those they call Amazons – never write things down. But – there's no escape. Breeding, Lalix. If they don't procreate – the root dies, the branch drops. If they multiply – it's with some Scythians, filmmakers, guys in dirty undershirts.... They're gone. There's their kids, on the corner sniffing glue...'

'Oh well,' says Lalix, not put out. 'If that's the way it is – we'll do what we can and must – then, in a year or so, we'll disappear.'

'Identity politics – it's *vieux chapeau*. Forget the gender stuff – call yourself an Amazon, and forget the woman stuff,' Corinne says.

'I'm confused,' says Lalix. 'I don't go with what you do. It's too ambiguous. Guys who are to fight must eat, and leave the camps. Then – they're something else, what they do is not confined, locked in.'

'They are more free,' Corinne says. 'That's why you do it – have them be strong, do what they want, and then to have a hold on them. Eats – material: then, a polity, symbolical. And everything they do, grateful, derisive – you are their avatar.'

'You're my mother, and I am super-loyal...' says Lalix. 'Though, now I find you're not my parent, there is some Firmine instead... Is it a difference?'

'No,' says Corinne. 'No difference. Your loyalty, Lalix – looks good on you. But – it makes you weak and vulnerable. It corrupts. Get rid of it, or bear it always on your back, like a fine putrefying animal you shot....'

'I maybe want like you, Corinne,' says Lalix. 'But on a bigger scale....'

'There is a pantograph,' Corinne says. 'That will fix the scale. Remember – cross me, and I'll know how you got big and puffed – a gadget. Watch yourself!'

*

'The singing! The drumming! Where's it come from, when there's no one there?'

'It comes from my shoe, cretin,' Marjane the Amazon tells Lalix. 'We don't go in that alleyway! I hear the words clearly, "thin people, at last they gorge: must let it all out – make little countries – rafts rolling downhill on shipwrecked skulls for wheels".'

'Shoe? What shoe?' asks Lalix wildly.

'Forget it, Lalix,' Marjane screams: she's distressed. 'Out! Let's get out, quick!'

It's hard and heavy. Shamans' drums. The words don't promise good. Someone left them on, to spin out by themselves.

There's no one round but those two comrades, they want to make it happen, all on a universal scale – not penury and weapons, but enlightenment, all over – some kind...

'You must be free to roam,' says Lalix. 'If there's a dirth – there must be rosemary and carlines, boil them up....'

'These don't look like houses,' Marjane says, shivering. 'Though people live in them.'

'They're lucky,' Lalix says. 'That those are not their houses. Anyway – we're not destitute, Marjane.... We're here for that, to put it right...'

'It's good,' says Marjane, 'to share. I bought an arm for our defence – it took our cash, every bit – but luckily – it doesn't work....'

There's silence. Lalix says, 'We find the network – that's what Corinne does. Or we weave it. Make the call. Then, the guys who help, and have our vision – turning little places into one big one, the people ... they show up.'

They walk around – this, they think, is the wrong way to start – 'I had the big idea,' says Lalix. 'But – something jogs you, and on the floor, it breaks, a crystal bowl, and yet, Marjane – you are the thinker. You follow it all through. The world is one, they say. You see that it is so. Chocolate wars and elephant deaths ... people who move, the fields they leave, plantations that arrive, and then it grows, a quantity, it's worn or eaten, walked on as carpets, a crust of red insects, ground into a tint in paint... I see the whole, but you, Marjane – you see how the parts have made it up....'

'I should have prepared more,' says Marjane. 'My head was ready, not my feet. Don't go down the alleyways, Lalix....'

'It's all alleyways,' Lalix says. 'Here, they're all women, all Amazons. They don't see us – it's all those kids. Look at them, all bundled up and flustered, like that, you'll never draw a bow. What shall we do here, Marjane? I remember people dancing, in the mountains – they'd had everything, then they lost it all, and that's how they knew what they had had....'

'That's not the way to see things, Lalix,' Marjane says. 'We see, without being seen – it's a disappointment, probably a copout too – but that's us, here. If you only seek what you have lost, looking in that little rearview mirror, where you never see your face, just your hair, never what's to come – the crash, the grey mountains, your grey hair.... it's not what you have had, that miniature, shaking with the movement....'

'People confident, dancing and revolving very slowly to applause....' Lalix interrupts. 'It's in that movie. I bet it's playing on a loop untended in a room near here....'

'Don't stray,' Marjane says. 'You're straying, Lalix: forget the movies, don't go near the alleyway, just stay in the one we're in.'

'We can't leave it, not like that, it shouldn't be our message, an epitaph,' says Lalix, 'that we weren't ready, not enough.'

'It's not the summary, Lalix, not a conclusion – it's just what we have here, in front of us,' Marjane says, 'Not our fault. I expect the people who's left here – they think they have a universal, and they suspect it doesn't work. The trouble is, I'm so attached to you, you and your family, all obsessed....'

'I love you so, Marjane,' says Lalix.

'It's not the time for that, Lalix,' Marjane says. 'Achille and Dominic – they said the same, but you're exactly what you'd be if you'd not met any one of us.'

'Isn't there somewhere we can plug in?' Lalix asks. 'Even – ask for advice?'

'It's always the same movie that they're playing,' says Marjane, lifting some sacking, opening a fine room – 'Those leopard cushions – could they be real? And what advice, Lalix? We had our plan.'

'Those big screens playing – they make it all seem more unreal,' says Lalix, 'The crew – must be shooting just around the corner – look! Isn't that us?'

'The carpet!' Marjane says – 'They should have hung it on the wall! Those stags! They've not been real round here for years....'

They wave at the small eye looking down from the wall, then look at the screen. 'Yes! There we are,' says Marjane. 'Will they come and rescue us?'

'Maybe we can eat from that big fridge,' says Lalix, pointing past the carpet, the hangings... 'I could eat flesh, Marjane!'

'No!' shouts Marjane. 'Don't open! We're not there yet! Let's go back the way we came, from when we didn't recognise the place's name.'

'Mother would tell us what to do,' Lalix says, 'Though she doesn't do fieldwork. Here, they must have power – it's all rocking on....'

'They'll all be in a building,' Marjane says. 'A temple. That sort has cellars.'

'No,' says Lalix. 'The open's always better. No floor to fall on you.'

'There'll be a coffee-house,' says Lalix. 'There is everywhere – though, did you read, it can't be grown in Africa? No more – climate, and growing other things.... The old men congregate, unless they're being carried somewhere even safer....'

'They might be eaten,' Marjane says. 'You think of young ones being tender, but the old ones are expendable, and what else can you do? The ancients thought grass was like flesh....'

'Don't even joke, Marjane!' says Lalix, laughing despite.... 'Besides, those old guys would talk you out of it. Think of all the pills they take!'

'It just takes a little,' Marjane says. 'One in a thousand – they get through, survive, and soon it's party-time again.'

'You're right,' Lalix says. 'It's gone quiet. Panic over. The guys will be off at work – those long fields.... I'll just go down, take a peek – that alleyway....'

4

MARJANE, RÉGIS & CLÉMENCE

'LIFE IS SUPERFICIAL, Marjane. That's its worst – it cracks when you lift it to take a closer look. But that's its best too – you're free to pass on. A life ends – but not for you. That's your truth, others go in the hopper – but you're still here. Here. Maybe there's nowhere else, but... A burning bush, you'd say, but even brighter: white light switched on, night never the same again... The humped field where they fought and cogitated poetry... they're gone, gone, gone under – and with us forever, that's our ground, our earth.... All wisdom, Marjane! I know it's heard and forgotten. So much taught. So much to come. It's all true, Marjane – and it's all the wind – blows in your face, and disappears, goes round the world, touches the rose in Isfahan, the kashmir sheep turns its back to it – then ...

here it comes again! fresher, fuller... When the life has gone – we see the meanings, the patterns. It's up to us: appreciation of the soul... They're all around, like pots in a museum. We don't recognise a soul, it's like a cast – the inside of something thin, familiar – a coat, a trumpet, a bottle. It's solid – but of course, you can't wear it, play it, drink from it. It's useless. But it's there....' Régis puts out a hand to her, then pulls it back.

'Lalix didn't share that,' Marjane says, provoked to tears, 'None of it. That broken stuff you talk about....'

Answering like that, though – it shames the comforter. It's not done.

'Lalix advertised,' says Marjane. 'She wanted a friend. I was the brightest, not the most understanding. Intelligence is a curse, of course. We know quite well how everything will turn out – but she attracted me. Free travel. A mission, and a message more intricate than "God is love". You'd discover things they couldn't take away. Your cash, your house, they can take those, just sitting at their screens. Not the whole house – the roof, say, or the floor. They read what you read, read what you write, unsmiling. That's what they do, from their box in the corner. But what you think, what isn't on the tape – that's yours. That's why I went with Lalix....'

'You don't have cash, Marjane: nor a house,' the guy, Régis, says. 'You're not a privacy freak? After what you saw....'

'It's states,' says Marjane. 'Tribes and gangs can get you too – but just now, it's states. States got scared – fighting each other's risky, but the truces mean they grow and grow – the fighting's back to tribes and gangs. They'll do the fighting, but the states – they grow and grow.'

Régis thinks Marjane is very clever, or very superficial.

'Lalix told me she did what she did to be bigger than her mother,' she says.

There's no reply to that.

*

Marjane thinks – 'I can be as large or small as I want. It makes no difference. Thin as a banknote dropped in a crack, or fat as something that blocks the pipes. Our poor dead, forgotten sooner than seems possible – death's an infection that might kill us if we let it linger round.... No sacrifice – that's good, good for the favourite horse at least, the servants too that we don't have, who won't be strangled, thrown down in the hole ... assuming we're all chiefs, princesses, no one grudges all the gold that's tipped down in our tomb....

'At least for Lalix, I should do something, a sign – I can't cut off my horse's ears, the tips, but I could cut myself, like on the steppe they do. I cut my ear – and how it bled, it couldn't stop, it was all set to empty out my head. Is it a circle, life? A straight line, a dot...?'

'It doesn't matter what you do, Marjane,' says Régis. 'Not a jot. You can try everything – you won't hurry anything along. The big change? It's in the book ... there it's stayed. I'm sure it fired you, pushed you on, and

Lalix too. The Manifesto – it was the dream that finished his first part off, that saw them swept all away, the fusty ones, bosses, the ancient prince: small cannons facing all of us, but reluctant to bang off. Democracy and socialism. That was the idea. Then came the fascists, Brumaire, long centuries of them. No dreams: those are structures. Then comes the long wait. The system ought to reach its end – is this the one, the contradiction bringing it to stasis, the sticking moment? Then the dream, at last, would kick in, become real... The change, the great change!

'It isn't so, it won't be so. There's no rites left. Even dancing round the pyre is out – they've all been tried, nothing works for death, Marjane, when it's dead, just leave it, leave it be, to not be.

'Nothing works for you, Marjane. You have to be a nomad, but it's hard, the hardest life.... That's how it was, and now, it's harder still, there's human sacrifice, of course, but there's no tree of life, there is no gold for you. There are no animals to shear...'

'It's not at all like that, Régis,' says Marjane. 'Nothing shakes me, nothing teaches me. No death, no politics, no life-circle. No nomadism – none of that for me. I never read Marx, I avoided it, it's a needle, it's a pill – I knew if I fell into that, I'd never shake it off, it clings like skins. Addiction's in the family, like for Lalix too – we didn't want to get ourselves hooked on that old man. It's like you said – the first life is fantasy, the second's waiting for the end: it's the Ramayana back to front. We went looking for something different – the one world given to us ... already there, just waiting....'

'Always it's the same,' says Régis. 'Always you end sleeping on the ground.'

He reaches out a hand, and again lets it hang empty, untouching, in the air. 'Of course – there is transition. It goes on for centuries. Hybrids too – feudals and slavers, factories, plantations – you can find a space, hang like a bat in some dark spot – it's not the great change, Marjane. You'll be long dead – and when it comes, it will seem natural, eternal ... quite mundane. If it comes when all is ruined, poisoned – you would not rejoice – everything grinds on, Marjane, men and machines, women making labour power: it's raising turtles, building pyramids, spotting winners... You're not made for that....'

'We wanted it all now,' says Marjane. 'I still do.'

She tells herself, 'Wait. Be prepared. You can be a leaf or a tile – leaves go into the shredder, tiles can't be ground – they break teeth, bone, gold or iron. There's not one ending better than the other. What does it matter, where or how I sleep? Lalix was exalted – overcoming every obstacle, sharing lives and liberating – then brought down by chance. I'm waiting, that's all, not resisting, not sustaining. I know it all – my time has not yet come....'

'I shall be a bat,' says Marjane. 'Thousands of us, uncounted and unseen. In the dark. Invisible, black against the black universe. Clever too....'

'Clever for yourselves,' says Régis. 'You're inedible. You'll never make it to the light. The only ones who care – are tiny insects, your food: – unless, of course, you're rabid. Maybe you assassinate?'

'There'll not be workers with a flag,' says Marjane. 'Just very young sick people inheriting a ruined land, not knowing how things work, and sick with nickel in their blood.'

'They'll eat you bats,' Régis says. 'Cannibalism would kill them off, and so it's you they eat. Me – I'll be a speculator. Become rich, and bring it all down, burrow from within....'

'Are you corrupt, then?' asks Marjane. 'I suppose you are. Your questioning, the contempt, contempt for answers not your own.'

'Oh, there's always signs,' says Régis, impatiently. 'The scene changes. Those suits of armour with the damascening – costly, ineffective. Steam engines in the fields – their chimneys like the funnels on the Aurora... No more muslins – sleepless nights for all tucked in those hedgerows, as modernity tramps heavy on all night.... Not that I would see all that. My work? – I leave the things switched on, they're owls – they tidy silently, my! how they work, without a screech....'

'You must believe ... something: in what is, was, a future if there is....' says Marjane, put out.

'I believe in what there is, happened, real, and nothing more. If you mean invisible belief – no!' Régis says. 'None of that. I had a bond with Lalix, not her projects. Body to body, that was us. Believing what you may today – tomorrow it's gone, into its hole. Gone away. Belief is water, waves. Abstracts – they don't count, Marjane.'

'You must believe in truth, even if you never tell it,' Marjane says, sceptical.

'If you do, it's underneath. It's a what-might-have-been, the wheels run over it, it's flat, Marjane,' he says. 'Think! Truth – it's like looking for causes. What's happened has had a sufficiency of cause. One doesn't matter more than any other. What's there's there, an effect: caused. Poking, stripping it down, won't change what's there.'

*

'You can't drink beer up here,' Amy the hostess says. 'Go downstairs, there's corners, people to talk to. Don't hang around in the bar up here, ogling.'

'I drink lots of beer,' says Régis, resisting. 'Don't worry.'

'It's your quality,' says Amy. 'Not how many. Down! Find someone who'll talk to you.'

There's a shaky stair, curled like a screw. 'Those are lovely beads, Lotte,' Régis says. 'It's etched carnelian, and blue glass spacers – looks like plant juice came in somewhere in the ovening....'

'Don't smarm your way in me,' says Lotte, holding up the necklace and squinting down.

'Oh,' Régis says. 'It's not that. I have a strong relationship going forward. Even stronger than the one I had before.'

'How come you know about jewellery? If you're gay – I love that. You can have a proper talk with gays,' says Lotte.

'I read a lot,' says Régis. 'All over, beads are the most common grave goods. Everybody used to wear them, once they were invented. Men stopped when there was capitalism – I can't think why.'

Lotte moves away, although she's curious. 'You should drink shots,' she says. 'This place is not for beer.'

Régis knows he should offer her a drink – it's what you do, but he doesn't do it. He's keen for some transaction with Lotte – he's no idea what, what she expects, is there for... 'Are you waiting for someone?' Régis asks.

'Oh yes,' she says.

He might offend her, or he might disappoint her. 'I'll see you another night,' he says. 'We'll finish this off then...'

*

'It's a pity, Régis,' Marjane says. 'With all you know, you get nothing. Not in the market, that's for sure, and you find nothing elsewhere that you want. Not that's paid. If you want action – that is never paid. I'm moving on. With my friend Clémence – we're trying to get money, for a project.'

'Not from Corinne?' asks Régis.

'Obviously not,' Marjane says, and laughs: 'Don't make me laugh.'

'You should try Jordan,' Régis says. 'I met a lovely Palestinian from there once – she said, "They don't look kindly on us. We are too many..." There are nomads too. They live real well, take tourists for a night or two, sleep under the stars – to see the rocks. There's a civilisation of boulders there, just lying round. That's where you'll find the secret of the stone age. Quite remarkable – it takes some brain to see what they are all about, the pattern, the design – why everyone moved on.'

'I didn't think there was a "why",' says Marjane. 'You wait, play every number – then it's all different. It wasn't up to you. First, it's stones, then it ends like now – in air. Voices, messages. Worse. Foul air – of course, air's just a gas, but you might say the air went lethal. The wrong kind of gas. You get accustomed, but it's always in your eyes – like when a theatre curtain rises, and you feel the cool air off the stage, the makeup, the acetone. You can't turn that around, you have to wait and hope – you can't think what comes next. It's like you said, Régis: "morbid effects". The world is pregnant, can't bring forth. The left, the right – there must be compromise, they say, and so no one gets what they might want. What they deserve.'

'That's just a trivial part, Marjane,' says Régis. '"Want, deserve". That's adolescent stuff – it's like you make a bond with someone young – seeking the youth you missed; or older – wanting the parent who lacked something. The search, always starting over, always at the start and always vain: always the lover, sought, never achieved. Why? Are you surprised, Marjane, how the lover never shows? Then you grow up – and wait: and wait.'

'That's what I thought,' Marjane said. 'Then I got bored with that as well.'

*

'Stages?' Clémence asks, derisively. 'You mean – democratic militarism, feudal jousts, then global war? Forward to the nineteenth century? Bird's beaks and layers of rocks? No God, no hero, no spirit – history erect like a totem pole, waiting to be topped out?'

'I'd guess you are an actor, Clémence,' Régis says. 'You have the cheeks for it.'

'Oh, I've had a strut or two,' says Clémence, flattered. 'I'm a philosopher really. On the boards – you need to follow dialogue. So – you're in Plato's cave, or at his dinner table – the lights that flicker, ghosts, or there's puppets, backlit... In the wings, though – it's Augustine. You fall, you climb to sainthood. Those wings don't lift you up. You tremble in the dark – then – it's you! walk on – there's light! There you are, in display, a diamond, cut and shiny. Us on stage – what do we seek? Why, of course! it's love, love of the people. Love, Régis, isn't gratifying, though. Love's not of the body, not what normal people want.... The desire and pursuit of flesh –

you land it, and it doesn't satisfy. You go on, go further... a climax without sex.'

She would expand, but Régis says: 'I don't recognise your thoughts, Clémence. Marjane's a sober type – you're talking of a fix that lasts for ever. This project...?'

'Oh don't be such a pillar, Régis,' Clémence says. 'You're a punisher! We're off to see the stones, and further still – the primitives, their happy lives. The Bakongo – they have a word for "leaving a mark"! That's cool – we'll go there. The early people – they take life as it comes, and, while it lasts – it's mostly good. We write it down, then people climb down off their stage, travel afar, and bring in what they left – slavery, wage labour, hermits. Rats, cats and measles.'

'Excuse me, Clémence,' Régis says, 'But that sounds facile.'

'Yes,' says Clémence. 'It is. That's me. And that's how most things are. The cleverer you are, the easier everything becomes. If you're a dummy, putting on your pants is complicated.'

*

'A dear friend gave me her,' says Lotte. There's a big illuminated figure by her door: 'Betty Boop'. 'She waits for me. She's lit up. Plastic.'

The room is very warm. There's a diploma on the wall – no, it's a sentence: 'The propositions of logic are tautologies.' 'I love him!' Lotte says: 'Then he denied everything he'd said before! Wow! That's brave!'

'I can't stay long,' says Régis. 'I see what you mean, though.'

'It leaves you free, free to do something else,' says Lotte. 'Something not logical at all.'

This room has no chairs – you stand around, it's like a bar. 'Have a drink, Régis,' Lotte says. 'A juice? Plant? Mineral? Once all those colored drinks were called "minerals", "mineral water". An odd idea – crush a rock – there's sand.'

'I'm here, Lotte,' Régis says, 'It's your birthday, so....'

'You're still here, even if it's not,' says Lotte. 'Most other people won't show up – is there a birthday logic too? That tells you who and where there is?'

'Don't take this stuff you read so serious,' Régis protests. 'Besides – it's me should have brought the drinks, to celebrate.'

'Yes,' Lotte says. 'You should. So, what's to become of you? Do you know why you are here? Or why you wish you weren't?'

'It's true,' says Régis. 'How my presence might turn out – it's absolutely mysterious. No one knows. If you're that way inclined, suggestible – it might disturb....'

'Jordan? Rocks?' Lotte asks. 'How they aligned six thousand stones, just using string, a loop of wire, with prehistoric animals around – and all that sex you say you had – Lalix? Marjane? And did that leave some mark, some sign? What difference would there be between a lively fantasy and some encounter half forgot?'

And Lotte dusts down Betty Boop, waits for the answer – 'Well,' Régis says. 'Those animals, I dare say they weren't prehistorical....'

'Of course they were,' says Lotte. 'If they were historical, we'd know what all those stones were for. And, Régis – leave those tales of sex aside – come in the kitchen, where there's chairs... It took millions of years to invent those – and maybe in a generation, there'll be no more use for them. Sit, tell me, while we wait for others to arrive, what you expect of me, what you believe... And – lying: that upsets everything, as you must know.'

'It wasn't sex,' says Régis, colouring up. 'It was relationships. Those too – don't leave a sign. Some people die, and others fall away – there is no mark.... I think, Lotte, you muddle everything up, though as for me – I think you know about me, but – what does that amount to?'

'You'd better stay,' says Lotte. 'Until you decide what it is you want, and if this capitalism can provide for you, or if you are enlightened, or a humanist – and if we each see colours in the self-same way and if we'll ever know it. You see things red, but I might see them beautiful as well. Red's often seen as beautiful – my *krasnyi* leaching into my *krasivyi*, my Red Army not a red at all: and redwood, rather reddish-brown....'

'That isn't quite the point at all,' says Régis. 'And capitalism – it doesn't come into that.... Nor what might come after, when I've gone. Ah! The new, the transformation – at once, familiar, a pain. 'What next?' they'll ask. Nothing to remember, told to "wait!"'

'You'd better stay, until you sort it out,' says Lotte, pushing Betty Boop aside, and getting ready to go out. 'Decide, Régis, and stay. Decide what you want of me, and how you'll know if you have had it, or anything at all. My party's in the bar....' and out she goes.

*

'Lotte was unique,' Régis tells Marjane. 'Not physical at all, but deep. Explorative. You couldn't get nearer to the silence. The point where all has stopped, and doesn't go on grinding on, destruction, creation, destruction....'

'I feel the same, when we have to take the plane,' Marjane says. 'It could land anywhere – even take you right back where you were.'

'It was an invitation to be her, that Lotte made,' says Régis. 'I was in her apartment. I could have become her, if I'd known anything about her, what she did, all that.'

'Maybe you should forget other people,' says Marjane, 'and yourself. Do something that excites.'

'I'm clumsy,' says Régis. 'This is Cité noire. I'd fall down a crack. I'm a cheapskate too – that gets you nowhere.'

'Right,' says Marjane. 'Stay in nowhere, then.'

*

He's hooked on that bar – they're unpredictable, the drinkers there. Someone follows him one night; he never recovers, not really. It's like falling off a motorbike, on your head – it makes you sweet and tranquil, as if you're on free painkillers for your eternity. It was passion did for him: that's the lesson. Passion for Lotte, who'd no time for him.

*

The camps beneath the plane are laid out like plantations. 'Poor Régis,' Clémence says. 'It seems inconsequential. Though – he's so pleased to see you now.... They broke his clock, in his head – he waits, but there's no duration. The roll is blank: you pedal, there's no sound. He's become a mystery – he's the only one who doesn't solve it: looking at him, you see at once the axe blows on his brain.... There seems no reason to it … no story....'

'Oh, it'll fit, you'll see,' Marjane says. 'It's modes of sedation – that has its history too, first the lobotomy, then the cosh, lead pipe or such. Wait, wait and see – the design comes clear so slow, but once it's there, it's like those chiselled stones – thousands of years, they sit, defined and sharp: two graven fingers up to your understanding....'

'Is this the country where we're booked?' asks Clémence, not disturbed – they glide like swans – loaded in, secured, hundreds of them....

'We'll find stones and camps wherever, Clémence,' Marjane says, her insouciance marks her as a true explorer, and Clémence falls in line.

'Régis is another person,' says Clémence. 'It doesn't work. Don't you try doubling up, Marjane. If the plane comes down – you'll find you are just one....'

'And maybe both of me will die,' Marjane says. 'And take the space for one. Compacted. Just one seat is ticketed. Besides, I've difficulty in being just the one. For me, each day is different, so am I.'

'Hmmmm,' says Clémence, testing the tarmac. 'What do I see? Oriental despotisms, with a touch of feudals, and some post- and neo-colonial hopes. A touch of theocracy, perhaps – and clash of empires – that goes on, I see, in minor keys, fortissimo. It's motor-cars, Marjane, that's where the interest lies. You don't need intellectuals for those – the admen tell you what to drive, and where to go, your representatives will have you grumble at the smog, the jams....'

'Quiet, Clémence,' Marjane laughs. 'I had all that with Lalix, and it ended bad. Now – there's the stones. That's what we came to see – not tents and slavery.'

'Yes,' says Clémence, 'there's nomads too – quite well set up – you go from camp to camp in four-by-fours....'

'Stones, Clémence,' Marjane says, 'we're here to see the stones.'

'Have you thought, Marjane,' says Clémence, 'that this could be the highest stage? The best that we can do? And after – nothing. Maybe start over everything – new body shapes, some underwater lungs, a touch of otter, something of the blushing octopus....'

'Of course I've thought, Clémence,' says Marjane, skimming through boutiques. 'Everybody has. You'll never know. What's lasting happiness is making your analysis. You can't have body fun for long – you live your life, a hobbled animal, scuffed deep with wear and tear ... you're in a fresco, or a book, you're flattened on the wall, the page. You're not in three dimensions – you don't run through the pricking grass, roar and shout, pick pineapples with your nose.... You're stuck in time, it doesn't yield a tick, a tock. Life, clockwork, Clémence, for us – is flat.'

'Yes,' says Clémence, hugging Marjane. 'It's stones. But – how I love you, dear Marjane...'

'I've no answer just now, Clémence,' Marjane says. 'I suppose a comment's needed. It's hot and sweaty here, even with no clothes on. Just imagine: the guys in skins – with no technology to waste your interest – you could do marvels with some stones – binary arcades! Each stone part of a computer with nothing to compute. Pure mathematics, Clémence...!'

'Compliments, Clémence,' says Marjane. 'Your skin – it's hardly used! When they say someone's soft as butter – they think of the colour, then the flesh. It's not the skin that's soft – it is the flesh. Like mozzarella. The skin, well – maybe it doesn't feel like anything at all without the flesh....'

'Those stones, Marjane – if they're not computers – they'll be maps – of everything you cannot see. Maps of destiny and origins. When we stopped hunting, then we became human. Between heaven and hell – there came the crops. Sitting and watching them sprout up or wither. Our worry, taking all our time, eliminating our cosmology. I think they let those maps subside – perhaps they buried them. Crops,' says Clémence. 'They grow like little people, every year you sow ... they're unpredictable, fractious ... kids who die, kids disowning you, kids rotting on the stalk. First – there was prey, the totem animals. Crops, though, are passive, spread out to the rain. The stones were navels, but coarse grains, farro – they're like us. One born every fall....'

'I'm sure we'll have ideas,' says Marjane, dozing off....

'When we stop being animals, what do we become?' Clémence wonders. 'Goat cheese and farro – it's a bread-and-butter question, I suppose.' She sleeps.

*

'Lentils,' says Marjane. 'That's what they discovered. That's how you live without the hunt.'

'Are you sure you got the country right, Marjane?' asks Clémence. 'Is Karnak in Jordan, or somewhere else?'

'It was all over, Clémence, everywhere,' says Marjane, irritated. 'Jordan is flat, so you could drag stones anywhere – no sweat.'

'You could read a book, Marjane,' Clémence says. 'And make up answers. Bed's cool. It's really hot, wandering around outside.'

'It's not that hot,' says Marjane. 'I know what you mean – it's the people. The camps. The stories. We can't go inside... Full-body exposure, it's called – you don't hear a bang. It sent those people into purgatory.'

'Don't be dramatic, Marjane,' Clémence says. 'This is the good part, this is safety, from some things. It's just not victory.'

'There's stones all over Turkey,' Marjane says. 'If you think I'm in error – you take over. Fly us there. What does it matter? – those days, there weren't borders. We need to spend our cash – be thankful it isn't from Corinne.... No one will come after us, to do accounts.... If there's some left, we could buy some people. Have them sent out. That's what you'd like, Clémence, that's what you think it's all about.'

'Surely we won't have that much left,' says Clémence. 'This room must cost....'

'How much do you think the people stuck here might be worth, Clémence?' Marjane asks.

They lie apart, angry: Marjane says, 'How ignorant you are, Clémence. You don't belong, wherever you are. How do you dare to travel? You're the last red ball, hard to pot: a stranger to each pocket...'

'That's good, Marjane!' Clémence says. 'You could sink me, if your eyes were set in straight! Your family – they're toxic. All of them, like you, hooked on to some kite ... some *farmakon*, a philter, incantation. Some recipe for stuff gone sour and stale. They live yesterday, perhaps tomorrow – nothing for today....'

'The old, dead guys, Clémence,' says Marjane. 'The ancients – are different from us. Did they think like us? How do we think? Thought's different when we write it down. I don't think the same today as yesterday, when I was younger. I shan't tomorrow – when I'll be old. The difference is – though we sit by the river, speculate in New Age Sufism – all that stuff – what makes us new is our analysis. If we think different – we know why. They didn't. They exist for us – we did not for them. Modes of production, that is why. We know how this society difers from the rest. Maybe the happy land won't come, with the next great change – but other stages there will be, hybrids, transitions.... When we think different – that is why. We totemise our pets, maybe we think that after death our nemesis will be our avatar ... just like the ancients did. But – these are fancies, nothing more. The machine – always the same – it's the brain, comes with the species, there is nothing else.'

'What nonsense, Marjane,' says Clémence. 'Of course they thought things different. And everything they saw was different, like where the sun slept, what made babies, who you should kill and who you'd dance with: – should you wear a pointy hat? or clothes? Or heft those stones and make a circle so the other guys could not see in... Time goes terrible and slow, so slow. They invent new gods, new things to fear, new endgames. Things that fitted, things that turned out thorny. Come on, Marjane! Think different? Of course – they do it now, they did it then. You're just afraid of going out and seeing all the tents and shacks.'

'If that is what you think, Clémence,' says Marjane. 'You should respect my reticence....'

They argue, then they quarrel – each thinks different from her pal.

'Let's go home, Clémence,' says Marjane. 'I feel bad. I think of Lalix, always.'

'That's terrible, Marjane,' says Clémence kicking the bed. 'You're letting everybody down – Lalix too – especially the dead and the condemned. A get-out to nothing, Marjane, nowhere, no ghost even – all the unheard, their rejected stories. You're stony, dear. You crumble in the sun.'

*

What have we resolved, Clémence wonders in the plane – was it about brains, cognition, old Marx, history? Stones? Or Lalix? Were we far apart – or was it the hotel, the tents – the bed...? It's ritual, all of it, especially the stones.

5

THE END

'YES, RITUAL: and bright things,' says Serge: 'When you ask, "What is man?" you could start there, listing preferences. Sharp tools too, of course – who wouldn't? – territory; boasting. Sulking, meditation. Second order stuff: – nothing special about behaviour. The day-to-day is standard, like hedgehogs. Prickles? – I saw Marjane. Without her sister, Lalix.'

'Oh,' says Clémence, 'they weren't related in that way. Marjane got cooked. She went with me as clay, came back a cracked pot. Herself – had seemed to hold a key – musical, not to doors. It was to colour everything. Instead – nothing. Silence.'

'Here's a paradox, Clémence,' says Serge, holding her tight above the elbow. 'I'm not tired of sex, sex with my wife though – I'm bored. The search for sex – is it idealism? The spirit – takes to its chariot....' She doesn't respond, but he assumes she's understood. 'In my work,' he says, 'the centre is the cities. There must be trees, a lake. Not the countryside. I hate the pastoral. The picturesque is finished, the unkempt countryside's gone. It's been transformed. It's industries – where you keep the animals, the food. You put the panels and the tents there. I hate it. It's a grid. You must have some green, even paint. Calming thought, Clémence: "a green thought ... in a green shade". In the city, it makes living easier. The rest, outside, is engineering. Saving animals, breeding them, perfecting crops. Think of the city as the stones. It begins with them. You needn't go beyond. The green grows up between the cracks, healthy and clean.'

'It's metals, Serge,' says Clémence, pulling away, not managing to break his hold. 'Iron to bronze to steel – the weapons are more refined. Rarer and rarer, names unknown to me, but metals dug up and rarified. They don't need blessing and belief – they work by themselves.... They're our farewell.

'The message – "don't dig too deep, don't use such heat..." "Don't pry into origins – you'll end up with a glimmer and some dust."'

'Follow me, Clémence....' says Serge, sure he knows the path. 'You must think in a new way, see what there is, and that it really is.'

'No,' Clémence thinks. 'The track's worn smooth. I don't want to be with him. He's right – so what? I don't want a happy ending, I want the ending to be happy.'

'Conventions, Clémence,' says Serge, letting her go. 'Respect them – the poetry, the philosophy, set out – look! the flowers, cut and dead on fussy tables, poor servants changing plates. The company – precious, voluble. But – don't linger there. You'll be at ease, but it's time wasted.'

'I see, I agree,' says Clémence. 'What do you want now, want of me?'

'Nothing at all,' says Serge. 'I want you to agree, to learn. Correct me, if you want. Your agreement, Clémence, lasts longer than anything else you give....'

'I'm not here to last,' she says. 'You're right, Serge. We can't call on the hoopoe for advice – if we want to last, we must love each other. The wise birds? – leave them in peace. Loving – it's a duty, but – I can't. If the species requires it, to survive – I'm not there, I'm outside the house.'

'You see, Clémence,' Serge says. 'I'm for the green.' He waves – beyond the walls, where you can't see, so far... 'The green revived. That's not my job, that's more important: it's the work I do. It's better paid as well.'

'I'm an ethnographer,' says Clémence, keeping up, 'That's why I was in Jordan. People and animals – they try not to meet. The scientific way – don't get attached to nature.'

'Oh,' says Serge, not quite giving up on something, maybe fun, with Clémence, 'I'm not with animals – it's buildings, low brick walls and such. I'm into those, the cubes and curves – the layout.'

'There's arks,' says Clémence. 'Beyond the street lights. Those places we can't go, where there are couples, two or more of everything, screwing behind the fences....'

'Oh, I have faith,' says Serge. 'Above all – in the wrath of God. It's terrible, it is the end. That's why I need Edens, as they are before the anger. Pest-free. I don't believe in good and evil, Clémence, and I hope you don't. That's where the wrath came from – the meddling with the animals.... An innocent choice – who knows what greyness it may bring you to? No good, no evil – that way you avoid the rage, the hurricanes, the lowering clouds....'

'It sounds quite crazy, Serge,' says Clémence. 'I'm sure it works as well as anything else. People like trees until they get too big.'

'Do you understand me, Clémence?' Serge asks. 'There's a whole lot more behind what I say.'

'I'm sure,' says Clémence. 'And it won't be humorous either. I come from a circus family – a pyramid, but we had trust and laughs.'

'Well!' says Serge. 'You must have muscles, in that line...'

'I don't mean in the ring,' says Clémence. 'I mean whatever each one did, there was understanding, not a hectoring.'

That shuts Serge up, for a while.

The serpent – was a joker – he didn't deserve his fate. It happens, when your boss thinks he knows best, and has no sense of humour. No sense of play. An original bad sport.

'The time comes for us all,' says Clémence, trying to let Serge down softly, but far down all the same. 'When we lose hope. It's like teeth – those go as well.'

*

'What joy!' Clémence thinks, as she drinks her big strong drink. Bars: so often places of liberation, not confinement. 'Serge! Not to have his face in front of mine, the mouth....'

That mouth! Marjane's silences! – what a movie they'd make, a primal Soviet film ... add a score, show the poor creatures in the fields, the scythe rising, the blade tinkling with drops of sun, and, framed, Marjane and Serge, never short of words or confidence, unless they were instructed to mouth silently .... scripted professions of faith and disbelief, to order. The scythe falls – no one is ever hurt, it's only montage....

'I don't pay,' she tells the barman. 'I'm a party girl,' and they both laugh.

In the movie she says, 'It's a revolution.'

It was happening as she and Marjane were in that room.

Scream!

We run down the Odessa steps.

We the participants; the spectators.

*

'I met Serge by design,' Clémence tells Germaine, who's older. 'He was one of the vague ones, with a pitch, a job, a badge that says he helps. He fixes poverty and moods

– but if you don't go with his display, it's a nothing nowhere that you get....'

'You don't need that, Clémence,' Germaine says. 'You need a good life, that's all. Don't say "we" run down the steps – pick out a person. Make us read his t-shirt, her broken strap....'

'That never works,' says Clémence. 'It's routine. I leave to you to say it's pointless.'

'We're in between,' says Germaine, not put out. 'Between the old life, when you were eaten by work and fatigue, and the new, where you're bored, sedated, and you want to knit your clothes.'

'I'm not there at all,' Clémence says. 'I'm gritty, like where I'd want to be.'

In the bar, there is equality, though it doesn't seem a starting-point. Jean-Jacques complained about his many friendships – 'More of a pain than a pleasure, owing to my friends' obstinate, or even perverse, habit of opposing all my tastes' – 'Exactly,' Clémence says. 'And I've a family, prostrate with addictions. I've the puzzle too – of sex indifferent to gender.... That's me! Dancing round the fire. That was my time. Sensation before everything, and there it ends, no attachment to the singular...'

'Oh no, Clémence!' Germaine says. 'You're not addicted to the drink – if you drink in company, you're just addicted to biography – your own. Your face – the bottom of the glass stares back at you. You're right – it's ritual, or its embers.... When we all danced and stamped together – this foul-tasting stuff was our bond, a tipple, no more. Now, we've lost the dance, and sit and drink the potion by the litre....' She drinks.

'That bag...' says Germaine. 'By your stool. It holds a life.'

'I'm between houses,' Clémence says. 'It's mine. We weren't paid for the stone ages stuff.'

'You should have adventures of some kind,' Germaine says. 'If there's any left. They often bring some cash. Anyway, you can tell me all you want. I shan't believe a word. No one here tells the truth about where they're going.'

'Great liars!' says Clémence. 'That we can all be. Illuminations! There are books of them!'

'How I envy you, Clémence,' Germaine says. 'The stones! Even if they threw you out. Jordan River! It goes through me like a knife, like – "baby, d'you wanna dance" – it makes my bones tingle. Jordan! I'm a Shoshone, pure as shit, through and through.'

'I wouldn't have known,' says Clémence. 'I'm nothing through and through...'

'That's a rotten thing to say, Clémence,' says Germaine, tussling with her. It gets hot.

'Leave it,' shouts Clémence. 'Leave that right now!'

The bag falls apart. It's a scene you've often seen, passed on by.

Jordan River often ran with blood – now it hardly runs at all.

*

'I won,' thinks Clémence. 'I shouldn't be pleased – but I am. Losing the bag, though – that's a pain.

'I've nowhere to go...
yet, everyone has a destination,
a family tree:
everyone's stuck up the teetering trunk
of their mangrove tree,
on the topmost twig,
watching the swamp
dry out below.
We're a child of the root,
all history's in each,
going back to the start,
then further still.
The childless ones – they teeter too,
but they're over and done:
and the rest, they cling on,
rise taller and taller,
babies sprout...
out of their heads....

In the beginning, seeds...
Fell from the stars.'

*

Clémence sits, bleeds, and sings the song. Before her, suddenly,

'Don't dream! Dreams is crumbs. Bread and butter pudding. Look – here's your bag.'

'That's kind,' says Clémence. 'But it's empty.'

'That's for sure,' says the benefactor, Flicka. 'It's evident.'

'I had a fight,' says Clémence, wondering who Flicka is.

'Oh, that's too improvised,' says Flicka. 'You're out, shot, shut. I'm a power rapper. I make you wonder at me, how slick I am, how I put you in my web. I can make you do anything.'

'Just now,' says Clémence, 'anyone can do that.'

'I do lots of things,' says Flicka. 'The trick is to do them consecutively. Do them all at once, you trickle out. All the time, I'm a philosopher. That's the only thing that gives you power today – it's not an institution, and you can see me, smell me, I'm not a hoarding, not a message, not a deadline, not a piece of news, not a form you fill in, not a machine, not a food that kills you or a poison cloud you've never seen, not a molecule they talk about. I'm not a person. I'm a skill.'

'Well,' says Clémence, 'the bag. I'll fill it one day, and you won't see how I do it.'

'It'll be crumbs,' says Flicka. 'Here, you'd better stop the bleeding – you won the fight, but now you're bleeding out. Here – smoke this, it'll calm you down.'

'I'm sure it's good stuff,' Clémence says, 'but I don't do smokes.' She takes it, though.

'There!' Flicka says. 'See? I made you do it – you saw I was good, and you trusted me,' and she skips and does a complicated set of steps to make a distance.

'Don't go! Don't go away,' says Clémence. 'Look at all this blood....'

'Do without me now,' says Flicka, waving.... 'If I stick around, I'll really hurt you, you could lose your life, and if you've money, I'll fritter it with you, we'll have a great time, and I'll move on. Now traipse, sweet nameless one, down your narrow path, and hope I don't come back.'

'She's right,' thinks Clémence. 'Not to copy anything. She never made a rhyme...!'

The place is rich – someone has dropped a slab of bread. You need that to stop the blood, like a poultice – it can start another life – press it to your wound, it absorbs as you forget...

'Don't listen to anyone: Flicka was right – that is philosophy....' and Clémence throws the smoke away.

'You'll never make it in the street,' the guy says – he's picked up the stub, and sniffed.

'I'm calm,' says Clémence. 'And – millions make it in the street, less educated too than me. I've a cosmology. Quotations. Bite and scratch. Love, hate – the whole repertoire.'

The guy – can't be a cop, or he'd have taken her, jail or hospital, accounting of the smoke ... probably a watcher, one who casts an eye. 'We all find someone to leech on to,' he says. 'Almost all.'

He goes on, 'Whoever designed you, he had something in his mind, for sure. It isn't clear: if you want refuge, you must ingratiate yourself, give someone the marrow of your life, a taste....'

'No,' says Clémence. 'Nothing with four walls, without a door. Just a door – that would do, and my stuff too, scattered somewhere in the road.'

Sergeant, he's called – his modest folks, in a modest state, thought that was the safest and most worthy rank. He writes immodestly on legal pads – 'a history of things' 'of people', 'of beasts', 'of all that's hidden'. There's thousands who do the same ... give dancing lessons too, hold your hand as you lie dying, follow, spy, denounce, win medals and encomia.

'I'll show you a place,' Sergeant says. 'Since you've nothing, they won't steal it. You can take what you want, though. Start again, build it all up. They had a project, the pair who started it, Russians I believe. Or Americans, adopted. It was a settlement, with a philosophy.'

'Oh,' says Clémence, 'I met one of those.'

'They have a garden,' Sergeant says. 'You must be careful – there are animals. Some you pet, and some you eat. You – you work, or else you plan. You steal, or you are stolen from. You are a colony, all of you, so if you don't have stuff to steal, you starve. It sounds a bit like – well: social credit? New economic policy? It's not the leap, I know. There's nothing sudden, risky. You stay there till you're sorted out.'

'Oh, I haven't time for that,' says Clémence. 'These experiments – they don't end well, but burning out – it takes an age. You're not the travelling sort, Sergeant, so don't suggest a trip with me....'

'It's not my thing,' he says. 'I collect. I select, restore, and then sell on. It's done for love. My love – your beauty: beauty fades, but love's eternal – that's what they teach in school.'

There's beds. On the big screen – 'Quai des Orfèvres', and 'That's a Khnopff.' Clémence says, 'Those are by Baj' – 'Comrades,' says the lady who presides, 'are encouraged to frequent museums, and such. Lay your bag there – you'll soon fill it up. Of course, most people like bright things – the paper note gets crumpled and is lost.'

In the cloister they're playing 'Le Grand Macabre' – 'You could hand round the cakes,' says the lady. 'Pots from Raqqa – that's the reward, they should suit, though it's modest – like Sergeant, our brave little soldier here, the most modest of them all....' and she squeezes his buttock and tickles his nose.

'I guess we have lockers....' says Clémence – the other two laugh. 'There's galleries, there's strongrooms,' says Sergeant. 'You see – it's the family tree. Like in the song. The bright things – they grow, just like fruit, and it doesn't seem just, how only some get to pick them off.... After all, we're all hungry, not just the farmers and the lairds. People here – they are aesthetes, they're worth milliards, they do deals on the side and make bets – there's just one bad feature, Clémence. Like the world on the outside – you can find one day, you've lost your whole stake. The bag's empty, you must start collecting anew ... but of course – the show, up on the screen, is for free, high quality; it runs all the time, never repeats....'

'Hmm,' Clémence says. 'I'm not sure. It's not quite for me – the company, maybe – won't suit....'

'They're ingenious, like you,' the lady declares. 'The comrades. Booms, revolutions and scams – economic miracles, gold rushes, hunger marches.... Comrades! – they're all noble of sentiment, committed and loyal – just like you thought they should be in the past....'

'Yes,' Clémence says. 'The past, how true. "*Vieux jeu*" springs to mind.'

'Well?' Irina, the fine lady, asks. 'Think – if only my countrymen had called me to save the Revolution.... Are you one of us, Clémence?'

'Hmmm,' says Clémence, tossing the bloodsoggy bread into a bin. 'It sounds delicious, stimulating, but it isn't me. Too risky. Too much success. Too much downside....'

'Yes,' says Irina. 'You're the losing type. Poverty, the street. Encounters with philosophers. The path is in your eyes. The horizon, Clémence – alas, it's a fool's trick, a mirage. The world is up and down, not flat to be strolled along.'

'You see, Irina,' Clémence says anxiously. '"Down" means only one thing to me. It's where the dragons stand, you pass through them, the jaws, the smokey fire, the rasping anus, and go further down to where you don't come back. When they hunted, when they killed each other, the forefathers – if you won, you stayed on the level; they went down. I know it's ritual, but it's still lodged somewhere in me – like, I hate the sea – it's down, and the water, obviously, it's further down again.....'

'Of course, my dear,' Irina says. 'It's poetry, and you are picturesque. But – it doesn't make a grain of sense, a smudge of difference.'

'That's what I feared you'd say,' says Clémence. 'I know, I know all that. and – you can keep the bread – it's not a metaphor or anything.'

'Of course,' says Irina, kissing her. 'You're afraid. We all were. If you're an addict – "up" is scary, you know you'll tumble. "Down": we've all been afraid. of there. Think nothing of it, we've all been through it...'

'The jaws?' Clémence laughs nervously. 'Through them? I don't believe it.'

'The fear, the combat with some foe unknown – we hope we won, we hope they didn't die and take our place, become a nemesis, and slit our clothes so that who knows what or who could creep in at a hem, poison our wounds, lodge with us,' Irina says. 'Of course, it's only ritual belief, my dear – carry on, along your path, and hope it's flat, without a mound, a drop.... Where might it lead, I wonder? The fear – does it grow less, since on a flat path, you can see everything around, no one can sneak up...?'

'That's exactly it,' says Clémence, feeling foolish. 'The street – you know precisely what there is, the unexpected's chronicled ... there's movies, chases, pistols, whores and pimps, series – even stretching out for years, flat as the Gobi, the song that jiggles you from here to there and back, up rise the pictures made of air, women and lions, griffins and cockerels, they're only stencilled on, balloons and cut-outs: it's small change, everything, the sex, the robbing, pills and smokes – it doesn't add, compute, nothing takes off for long, it all falls back, flat, Irina – flat as the cops' flat hat, the *blin*, the hangover, waking, your lower parts encrusted with a rosy salt ... where were you, what did they make you do? It's of no consequence, nothing's original at all....Up you get, it all starts, over, again, without an end....'

'And that's enough?' asks Segeant, though he's heard it all before. 'Enough for you?'

'If not, I'll tell you, I'll come back....' says Clémence.

'No!' Irina says. 'You won't come back. No one has, not ever. Stay – or forget me.'

'I must seek out,' Clémence starts, weeping, as they all are weeping now, '– what it is that you don't know, and what you insist on telling me about, having me accept, adopt, immerse myself. Flat, up, or down – it's not enough, even if – it's all there is.'

'No,' says Sergeant, pushing her out, along, by the shoulders. 'I think we're at this point – intense, deep relationships, not friendship though. I think you'll like where I am taking you – the House of Corrections, maybe you've heard...'

'Lovely!' Clémence says. 'Dostoevsky. The movie, probably quite short; and corrections are always welcome, if you don't take them seriously.'

'It doesn't do to be too serious,' says Sergeant. 'Relax! When your clothes are off, they'll tell you what to do – a giggle, that will help.'

'Hey!' Clémence says, wriggling away and running up the street. 'No military stuff for me!'

*

'Free!' Clémence whispers. 'I know that anarchy is wrong, a measle of the spirit, infantile ... but how I enjoy – no handcuffs, no one looking down my top, my bottom, torching my shack, running off my sheep ... instead, the revelation, husking, stripping down – a figure "one", bending and skipping in the wind, unique.... And I forgot! – sewn in my clothes those carnelians, the lapis lazuli, the turquoise, that we bought from shady guys in Al Jizah.... Authenticity – either it all is, or there's nothing...'

Stones. They ought to save Clémence. She has the jargon – a copy, of what the shady guys passed on – and on and on the stones will circulate, drab, contrasting with the fine spiel accompanying them.

*

'I'm unmarked,' says Clémence. 'I'm rid of all these – Serge, Sergeant, the rest. I've injured no one; those I can't ingest – Flicka, Irina – they slide off; I'm a sheer and shiny surface, formica.... The ant, industrious and clean. I begin, over and over, each time – fresh....'

'We all hope that's where we'll end,' says Masha. 'We all have lives exotic and mysterious – players of the lyre, snarling warriors, ascetics – liars – what ties us down and makes us similar, is birth identical and – especially – death, all different till the minute after.... I remember, Clémence....'

'Oh,' says Clémence, 'you flitted in and out, but we never adventured far together, Masha dear. You're a figure in my album, that is true – but was the album mine? Or handed on, a family, maybe they all ended in a pit, or lay beneath the fruit tree they so loved, limbs mixed and scattered, on the ground, waiting for someone to assemble them ... photos taken in a booth, canoodling with some person casual, pulling a face and grinning, or before a landscape painted, fake.... A precious ancestry, the archive – passed to wrong strangers, the silk stockings, worsted pants, frozen faces ... who cares, the thought identical as birth ... the record, any record counts and counts on...'

Masha doesn't deviate. She waits...

'All right, Masha,' Clémence says, sitting beneath the tree, hugging her knees. 'Tell me about me, about what I don't remember and don't tell.'

'When you were young, you had something of Romy Schneider,' says Masha. 'You were a firestick, a poker – very straight, you could make the fires of jealousy roar and squeak...'

'Jealousy?' Clémence says, acting surprised. 'What of? What for? Who was that person – Romy? – anyway?'

'Let me go on, this isn't a love story,' Masha says, overflowing with her memory. 'Since you ask – yes, Romy had something of the boy about her too, with the right makeup she could pass. But this, ours, wasn't a settled place – not Anatolya, though there were Turks for sure, and all the Turkish smells – tobacco, coffee – quite banal. And Greeks, Byzantines, Macedonians, and certainly Parthians and Kurds – Albanians – all seemingly mixed up, in this state that is no more, and hardly lasted ever, like an experiment of southerners – the Yugoslavs. Slaves, many of them, out of the darkness, not so many Slavs, I'd say. People who came from very far, steppe Turks, Scythians – who thought first, I wonder, of the horses, the sacrifice, the asmavedha, perhaps already an archaism, Vedic, when it was revived, or borrowed from the funeral rites... That horse, so full of hope, abandoned.... The mighty Guptas....'

'Ah yes,' says Clémence, feeling lost. 'The rites. I know those would enter.'

'...sorted into armies. First the fighting, then the armies...'

'I was a baby,' says Clémence, laughing. 'I might even not have existed. What then?'

'... the fighting – just swinging and cutting. Nothing organised, just following fear and anger, hitting out.'

'I know the army, the Yugoslav, made more movies, fought more wars in them, from Alexander to the Qarakhanids – more than any other. Then it fell apart, into these people who thought they were different but were all part of time, not of each other, but of things they didn't know, never could imagine...'

'So, where do I come in, Masha?' asks Clémence.

'Forgiving people of whom you know nothing for things you know nothing of, carrying your understanding foward to a point beyond friendship, to an intense relationship where you were inclined in the name of no one but yourself to condone, become an accomplice, from goodness of heart or transferred guilt, or simple attraction of evil, a disbelief in criminal intent or being drawn to it, in others, then in yourself....' says Masha in a breath.

'That's what they used to say,' says Clémence, 'but it's wrong. You don't know what you, or someone else may do, have done – in a blind, in black, in retro, constrained or willing, resigned, damned, terrified, exalted or indifferent ... a prisoner of their time, and wanting to be out of it as quick as possible.'

'I'm not a judge,' says Masha. 'I draw no conclusion ... I describe.'

'My poor resentful patissier,' says Clémence. 'I cradled him, my poor baby, the murderer. I had him suck my breasts. What revenge has the species excogitated for him?'

'In whose name did you forgive? Whatever he had done?' asks Masha.

'In my name,' Clémence says. 'Whose better? And where were you, Masha?'

'I was jumping off the rocks,' says Masha. 'Lovely sea! Keeping my innocence fresh and clean. And you went to Africa, understanding everything, watching close as all your mates snuffed one another...'

'Yes, maybe that was a mistake,' says Clémence. 'With that expanse of Africa, there's nothing to be done – we kept the anger to ourselves, abandoned friends, sequestered others: the indigenous – we left them to themselves. It was a blessing. For everybody.'

'There's no way back,' says Masha. 'The past – indelible, invisible. What might we two have done, in reparation or exacerbation?'

'How often must I tell,' says Clémence, 'that I am not a humanist. I ignore. Call it forgiveness. I can't pardon, no one can, so best not think of it. You pull the cart, or else you lie beneath the wheels. You pull, and you can sing – remember, it's quiet there in the ruts....'

'Be still, Clémence,' says Masha. 'I can help you. At this point, "help" means "I can save you". You know the worst thing about hell? It's not that you can be let up only for a day, to walk around, buy candy-floss and coddled eggs – food that all ghosts eat – and then go down again. No. The worst is – in hell, there is no devil. No one to make a pact with. No parole. No torture – how could there be? You have no nerves, no brain. It's just that: what it is. Hell. It's what you choose, have chosen, Clémence.'

'It would be worth to have you save me, then,' Clémence says, half scared, half laughing. 'They say there is a God – busy in his garden. Taking a stroll.'

'You want to play, Clémence?' says Masha. 'All right. They say – "God is love". That's it. A word. It's all there, useless to fiddle-faddle – the word was there, in the beginning. And in the middle and the end, you bet. Be grown-up, Clémence. Be serious – you're in the shit, you may as well acknowledge it.'

'Maybe – mischievous spirits. They're more credible. The rest – I'm sure I heard it all before,' says Clémence.

'Everybody did,' says Masha. 'Forget all that, we shan't get anywhere. I'm trying to give a hand, Clémence. Be like everyone – believe what you like. I'm talking about steps, next steps.'

'I run, Masha,' Clémence says. 'Run with me … big steps, kangaroo....'

'Yes!' says Masha. 'There's a scheme – so huge, if you are part of it, you only see the tiniest bit – it's bigger than our history, indeed, our history is tucked away, like in a corner of a drawer. The motor of the world, Clémence, is labour, mostly past, turned into cash, that you can store in walls, or under floorboards, lend to nameless guys, above all, cash in the abstract you can hide. Empire? A thousand years, the rising sun, the never-setting sun, whites on blacks, us against barbarians – all that? Forget it!'

'I already have,' says Clémence. 'I'll run with you and your idea – but I am flesh. Where do I fit?'

'Oh well,' says Masha. 'I said – this is all, total, history. You'd find a bridge that you must cross – there's slavery, or something like, there's soldiers in the streets sometimes, – but it's a bridge, Clémence. A road, a passage: obligatory, but one you take and then it ends, it's finished with. You're over. You're on the other shore. A phase, you must go through it – hunt, gather and enslave: an echo of the past. You're weary with the trek, but you are calm. You'll manage anything. Guys get these manias – their gods, their territory, hypotheses – it makes them go beserk, like elephants. It's species memory; they're manic, they regress.

'The only true belief for everyone is – money: gives security! Sane and silent, you amass, and you tell no one, raise no flag, coin no slogan, write no book.... Money – gives freedom, and it keeps you safe.'

They stare, Masha and Clémence: Clémence is impressed, and Masha giddy with rhetorical success....

'Cash keeps you safe, and steady,' Masha says again. 'That's the belief. It's false. Of course, it isn't true! We're built like robots – all those dangling limbs, the fiddly apparatus that we use for sex – the lolling heads, the short unhappy lives ... how could we be secure, with anything? Eternal need for fuel, repair... And Clémence, remember too, that you make money from the street, you don't make money *on* the street....'

'If I read you right,' Clémence says. 'You people unravel everything, the history, all that, you do a re-run of it all and then – you are demystified... But – the last, the highest stage, remains a competition for the cash – most money and least work, that is the goal. It sounds banal, dear Masha. How does that save me? It's all false, an illusion – you collapse it, on it goes! You think we're at a start again, with all our straggling arms and legs, our dirt, our maladies....'

'Not "a" start, Clémence,' Masha says. '"The" start.'

'But – I'd have done the risky stuff – been a slaver, been a slave, a soldier, prisoner, and victim too....' says

Clémence. 'And in the end – it seems I'm rich, but – there's no guarantee....'

'There is a way, Clémence,' says Masha, holding her. 'You end up rich, but – then, you give it all away! You're clean! Saved! That's what I offer you.'

'It means – I do all that you say: I end up poor, demystified,' says Clemence. 'And all the rest are rich but mystified... That's how I am right now....!'

*

She lets herself appear convinced. It isn't revelation – that comes next – but it's belief and trust. Dear Masha! All those fantasies, the longing and the wish...

*

'I must prepare to sum it up,' says Clémence. 'The whole whirligig. Us, now and after. Rites, beliefs, and obsessive practices. What they call the "consciousness of the consciousnesses", everything at the instant that we know: the collectivity, and all it knows.'

'Whoa!' says Masha. 'That's insanity.'

'Then, there's our saving feature, our speciality,' says Clémence. 'Sentiment, empathy. The boy, archaic, buried in the sand, a blue stone in his hand.... Adventure. The fiery furnace. Those Christians keen on burning people like themselves, marched in, redhot, faced down the lions... I'd think to turn to Islam too, it's hard, and confident, and sometimes beautiful: those ancient plates from Tunis, cemented in the church tower. Terracina – China's land....'

'Quiet, Clémence,' says Masha. 'Don't fantasticate – China hadn't been discovered then.... Get in your boat! Burn out your canoe – much harder than it sounds. Load it with beasts. Find two of everything, if you can – one will do, we'll clone it if we must, and seagulls, an albatross or two to keep the poetry in motion.... Water is everywhere, undrinkable, Cythera quite submerged....'

'The crack of those Aurora blanks, that I believed in once, now seem the snapping of the knout,' says Clémence. 'Here in the tall waves, there's coastguards; on the shore, the guys with rifles, driving us away, landfall and slavery would be best, and oh! these elephants, they breed like scorpions, there's no room, Masha, just no room.... The shore! Salvation! New life! But it's already populated....'

'The canoe was for a river, stupid,' Masha says. 'The history – get on with it! Remember, "the highest form of psychic life, embraces all known reality" – that chanting, and the coca that you need to take you into purgatory and back again, the jaguar skin, obsidian sword – no, it's not kiddoes' play, it's real; collective consciousness....'

'That's what I said!' says Clémence. 'But – you threw me in a wilful murky flood – a paddle's not enough.... We must have order, Masha: whole stages of production fall down around like thawed-out ice-shelves, volcanoes ahead and vortices behind – the cruel fish, tied legless in their element howl round the hut at night, my dog goes back to wolf, oh Masha....' Clémence cries... 'These are effects – before those, there's causes, so they say. Does that imply there's order? Logic? I am sceptical....'

'Touch it at once!' shouts Masha. 'The blessèd bone, the book of spells, the cross, the swastika, the vipers' knot – and shout! The beasts, the spirits, they're often frightened off by man's excess and rant ... besides, you know the hunt will do for them, they're on the slide, we'll eat their food and cook their little ones in pies – the higher knowledge, even science – that, is on your side.... Pray, Clémence, but not too loud, or you'll attract the neighbours, and they'll take your hen and goat, but as you drown or burn, you know you spun the wheel, and "*ting*"-ed the bells, you're clean, the heavens no doubt took your routines as proof of your obedience, wrote your destiny with circumspection – rebirth as something humble: or a spell in paradise....'

'It can't be all religion,' Clémence says. 'I don't believe a word, except for incantations on an enemy, who dies in frightful pain. Where is the rest, the good stuff we've amassed ... the true, the beautiful, the artisans' white jade and ormolu, my coloured stones?'

The canoe – drives forward – out of sight of her, there must be crew.

But – 'Oh Masha!' Clémence says, 'I hear your voice, it seems to me the voice of History. Am I obsessed with you? Are you the love I never had, was never capable of, and who avoided me....'

'No,' says Masha. 'I'm not History. I'm "might-have-been". We've all had lots of those. That's history too, but time, dear Clémence – time is not a tapestry, hung static on the wall, that you can snip bits out, stitch on a figure, or a fawn.... Time is a desert road, Clémence. I am a twisted tree. You saw me, and you wondered, longed ... inevitably, on you went, the traffic's tail-to-tail, dogged, at a constant speed... I was that tree: you can't go back and gather fruit from me....'

'Maybe I'll haunt and stalk you when I've done with this,' says Clémence. 'Now, what next?'

'Armies, libations, hecatombs,' says Masha. 'Down this rhyton of retsina, like the brave Greeks did, and hope it makes you wise as them.... Courage, my dear, and don't look back...'

'It's the bodies, Masha,' Clémence says. 'They're everywhere, in piles. Someone has put numbers on, there's so many digits on the card, they cover up the face....'

'Don't be flabby, Clémence,' Masha says. 'The plague-pit that we live in, it's the same one for all of us. Many guys got paid to die all kitted up, or else they had a herd, defended it: or thought they were too innocent to interest a foe.... Don't think of quantities – think of the many ways we meet our end: there is a variety so great, it keeps you on your toes avoiding it.'

'You are my guide, my hope, Masha,' Clémence says. 'Don't say I invented you...'

'You're a fly in my room, Clémence. You buzz,' says Masha. 'Should I squash you? Throw the casement open...? You're a penitent, kneeling at my frontier. If I don't let you in, you'll starve. If you get in – you'll be garbage. So, *ma semblable, ma sœur*, paddle! Row, pedal, stoke the boiler ... spur the nag....'

'I conclude,' Clémence says, 'that One God means one knowledge, some principles that would end in axioms. One world, one end, perhaps one species – has the key, the why, the whither and the whence. But life and history ... don't fit. Monotheism – it's a monomania. Spirits and warring deities make more sense. Could one have both – a species with the key that opens everything, then lives it as it all unravels, sees its own death and disappearance, leaving no creature that can read or measure, nothing that's interested in the unity? Or maybe neither... No principle that unifies, and nothing plural, consequential either: – just reproduction, better tools that kill the grass and dessicate the earth. Stones, designs, laid out to honour killer priests...'

'I'm not interested in all that,' Masha says. 'Stick to the script, Clémence.'

'I did,' says Clémence. 'One of our characteristics is not a love of truth: it is belief. Belief in something. Constant through history, is that need: belief, always destroyed, then, as time runs on, replaced. Each belief is false, exploded – on to the next! You could say too – every confession, however drastic it may seem – is false, consciously or not. Too little, or too much. Too much weight to moral hindsight, assured there is no reparation, only useless blame. Belief, assertion, all is false...'

'No, no, Clémence,' says Masha, 'I grant you all beliefs are wrong. It doesn't hold for each confession – if it were so, Nietzsche would self-destroy....'

'I hadn't thought of that,' Clémence says, abashed. 'It's better that I finish with the tale. The money question, dearest friend. An advance, perhaps, would be allowed? And, as for chance, belief and all the rest – let's think of earthquakes, and volcanoes too. Suppose a volcano didn't stop – an everlasting bleed, until the earth was empty and the crust collapsed: – what then? Or is that too Voltairian, dear friend? We've few beliefs to lose, except the one that says we shall go on, ever upward and inventing, creating disasters and the means to mitigate their consequences....'

'Well,' Masha says, 'I heard all this before. It's what that old guy said – everything you think you know's impermanent. If we are there when there's an end – we'll be together, just us two. It doesn't comfort me – maybe it comforts you?'

'The cash,' says Clémence. 'That would do for now – the rest is not poetic. It breaks right out of genre. If it is true, it isn't beautiful at all.'

'History, Clémence! Get on with it. It's judgment day; all's up to you,' says Masha.

Clémence has doubts. 'Masha,' she says, 'a future with you, your folk ... I'm not so sure.... The trouble is, Masha, you're a jealous crone. Obsessive, naive, and limited....'

'Clémence!' shouts Masha. 'That's obscene! That's what you tell your cat!'

'There's more adventure, lots more history that I see,' says Clémence, taking heart. 'From you – no contract and no cash.'

'You'll find that on the street as well, you dupe,' shouts Masha, pushing Clémence out, resolving though, never to let her go: force her to justify that mild rebellion ... haunt her, climb in through her eyes....

*

'Free again,' says Clémence.

'I love women,' Jackie says, plates of fried entrails before them both. 'I don't make ladies work for me.... Especially if they've family. Do you? ... Clémence?'

'Like everyone,' says Clémence. 'Every one – goes right back.'

Jackie seems satisfied by that: they unwind the insides, spaghetti-like.... 'The Greeks ate these to make them strong....' says Jackie. 'I'm hooked on them. They say they foretell the future. To me, it's the past they signify – they're works, like in a clock. Take them out – time stops. The Greeks – they didn't imagine anyone came after them! I love that!'

'And retsina?' Clémence asks. 'Then why bother drinking that foul stuff if it all ends with you? Anyway, I've not the body suitable for working on the street...'

'You see,' says Jackie, 'it all comes down – to a virginity. The Parthenon. There was a battle between Athene and Poseidon. In the night, Poseidon threw down all the blocks Athene put up by day: a sexual metaphor. And that is where they lie till now, the stones. She kept her purity – but lost the residence.'

'I didn't know that,' says Clémence. 'But it's true, Athene didn't go to school – she knew it all at birth, she'd done her military service too. She was knowledge – in the sea there's none of that.'

'How true,' says Jackie. 'Clémence! I bet you're out of luck – to look at you, you need a prod to set you going forward. If we were ancient, we'd invoke some god...'

'I know. I am a temple,' Clémence says. There's silence.

'I had the promise,' Clémence says. 'To get first rich, then wise and poor. I told everything, the history past, the future too. I was an oracle, ramped up, high as the sky. My friend – now, she knows as much as me, of why we're here, the what, whence, whither, all that stuff. Giant steps – but I missed out on the cash, and then the revelation; that comes after: the vanity laid bare, the wisdom gained.'

'It often goes like that,' says Jackie, giving a friendly touch to Clémence's knees: 'You're two steps short. But beautiful and cultivated all the same.'

'I know,' Clémence says, 'I deal with spiritual stuff that really doesn't count. The big change? All turned upside down? Not here, and not by us. I left it out.'

'It would not have fit, besides,' says Jackie.

'That's right,' Clémence says. 'Fuck off, Jackie. Now, what's your scheme?'

*

They don't work for Jackie, those ladies don't. They're self-employed, they make and do what Jackie says.

'Don't worry,' Jackie says. 'If there's great danger – the spacemen will come for us, winch us out, take us back up. They even look human. Home? A small planet, well equipped, discreet.'

Each day, Clémence starts out from a different room. The panelling is tulipwood, the doors to the next, larger, room, are always open. You go through, someone far away is planning. All our lives depend on it, that last room ... but there are pictures on the way, and tapestries, and gewgaws on small tables – put them in a pocket, they'd surely not be missed ... except, you don't have pockets. So, they've thought of everything!

They're talking of the soldiers' pay. And of their morality. Defences – they must be patched up, and there's the cannon foundry: the wood, the charcoal that you need, the sand, must be the right kind, river sand's too fine, and the iron, the brass fittings, more wood for guncarriages. The band: if there's too few, the instruments too small, it can't be heard, doesn't inspire ... and who shall write the anthems? Pay too little to the infantry – they'll rise up, desert. Pay too much – they'll settle into military careers and take you over. The people must be happy, and must be kept at bay. If you have to fight, it's because the others think you'll lose. If they're not sure, you'd do a deal – a truce, a satrapy, alliances – bribe a desertion, that's a ploy to try... And so they talk, but your path goes down, down under the kitchens, to where there's Alibaba jars, with dirty underclothes in dirty suds, grain overlaid with mouse-shit punctuation, crusted honey, the rancid fish sauce gone more rancid: stained bedcloths, livery jackets with the silver thread unravelled ... waiting, waiting...

Broken stuff.

Then up again – past heaps of carrion waiting to be stewed, and parts of beasts that's waiting to be thrown, out to the dogs.... And this seems to be the war-room – the ops, it's called.... Artillery maps, like children's drawings: corridors of retreat: flags, the castles for the elephants' backs, the throwing spears, the Gatlings and the Thompsons, all listed here. Jewellers' designs – medals, fans for the victory parade: the inventory for what will pay the victors' reparations: trunks to hold the ransoms if you win....

Outside, the gardeners go stooping past ... and there's an osprey!.... There'll be a pond... Where do the hoopoes live?

*

And when the dusk has turned to dark, real dark, Clémence sorts the work that's ready to be paid, maybe she changes clothes, to go outside under the lights.

Still two steps short.

About the author

John Fraser has lived in Rome since 1980. Previously, he worked in England and Canada.

www.ingramcontent.com/pod-product-compliance
Lightning Source LLC
Chambersburg PA
CBHW020548310726
48979CB00008B/1134/J

* 9 7 8 1 9 1 0 3 0 1 5 5 5 *